Heart's LOVE

D1086951

By Katharine E. Hamilton

ISBN-13: 979-8-9856240-3-8

Heart's Love

www.katharinehamilton.com

Cover Design by Kerry Prater.

All Titles
By Katharine E. Hamilton

The Brothers of Hastings Ranch Series
Graham
Calvin
Philip
Lawrence
Hayes
Clint
Seth

The Siblings O'Rifcan Series
Claron
Riley
Layla
Chloe
Murphy
Sidna

The Lighthearted Collection
Chicago's Best
Montgomery House
Beautiful Fury
Blind Date
McCarthy Road
Heart's Love

The Unfading Lands Series
The Unfading Lands
Darkness Divided
Redemption Rising

A Love For All Seasons Series
Summer's Catch
Autumn's Fall

Mary & Bright: A Sweet Christmas Romance

Captain Cornfield and Diamondy the Bad Guy Series
Great Diamond Heist, Book One
The Dino Egg Disaster, Book Two

The Adventurous Life of Laura Bell
Susie At Your Service
Sissy and Kat

«CHAPTER ONE»

"*And so, as you go* into this new school year, create an environment for learning that will leave your students eager for more knowledge!" The crowded auditorium erupted into applause as the lanky motivational speaker waved and exited the stage to stand by the doors at the back of the auditorium, shaking hands with teachers, administrators, and other school staff as they exited. Amy Frasier glanced down the row at her friend and fellow teacher, Aaron Jacobs. Catching his attention, she rolled her eyes heavenward. Aaron laughed as he made his way toward her. "You not a fan of this year's speaker, Frasier?" Aaron's dimpled smile lit his lean face, giving the harsh angles of masculinity a boyish charm that warmed his brown eyes to a soft caramel, which Amy knew typically drove the ladies crazy. Amy had known Aaron for six years, and not only was he her fellow teacher, but also her friend. The two of them had set out from college in Auburn, Alabama, to teach in the Dallas/Fort Worth area of Texas. Both native Texans, it made sense for each of them to move back to their home state and be closer to family, and with Aaron's connections at his alma mater, he and Amy had been a shoo-in for the open teaching positions. Aaron draped his arm over her shoulders and waved at a couple of their fellow team teachers as they walked toward the exit.

"I hate coming to these things," Amy replied. "Every year the information gets cornier and cornier."

"Character development." Aaron squeezed her shoulders in a light hug before releasing her to shake the speaker's hand. "I enjoyed it very much."

Amy rolled her eyes at Aaron's false statement and extended her own hand behind him. The man smiled broadly as he shook her hand. Amy said nothing, but politely moved on ahead.

"You couldn't even tell him good job?" Aaron chuckled as they walked down the locker-lined hall toward their classrooms.

"If I thought it was a good job, I would have said so." Amy's blunt answer had Aaron laughing even harder.

"You are a harsh critic, Ames."

She shrugged her shoulders as she grabbed her purse from her classroom and locked the door. She waited for Aaron to lead the way to his truck.

"It's a shame the new English teacher missed out on such a riveting conference," Amy continued dryly. "When does he move in anyway?"

The new English teacher, subject of the hottest gossip to hit the teacher's lounge, had everyone buzzing the last couple of days. Not only were the rumors of his charmingly good looks circling about, but also his unattached relationship status. Amy had walked in on a conversation the other morning in the lounge between Suzanne Smith, Home Ec, and Rosa Lopez, Spanish I, both giggling as though they were the high school students rather than of the teachers. Apparently both women had witnessed the new teacher signing his paperwork in the principal's office. Amy had acted unimpressed with their assessment as they babbled to her excitedly, especially when she found out the man would be Aaron's new neighbor.

She had yet to meet the mystery man, but knew Aaron had planned their annual teacher gathering at his place for that evening. Then, everyone would meet, not only the new English teacher, but all new teachers. Every year, Aaron hosted a large barbeque and party for the teaching staff at P.S. 14 as a last chance for all to enjoy their summer vacation before the start of school the following week. Amy, as best friend of the host, held party-host responsibilities as well.

Aaron locked his classroom door and swung his keys around his finger as they walked. "He moved in today, hence why he did not make the conference. He should be all moved in by now, though, which is great since people will start arriving around six and the moving trucks will need to be gone off the street." He glanced at his watch, his Christmas present from Amy that Christmas. "That gives us three hours to decorate, whip up sides, get the drinks iced down and the volleyball net set up."

"I'll swing by the store and grab the remaining groceries, grab my clothes from the house, and then head right on over, then. I figure I can work on the dips and trays while you set up outside." Amy and Aaron nodded at one another in agreement of their plan as he backed out of the parking lot and headed toward his small neighborhood not far from the school.

∞

"Amy, I don't see the problem." Rachel Cline, fellow teacher and friend, held the heavy glass door open with her foot as Amy carried two large paper sacks full of groceries into Aaron's house.

"The problem, Rachel, is that I don't have time to show a new teacher the ropes. I'm already behind on my lesson planning and I still have to decorate my classroom. Did I mention I'm painting this year?"

"Yes, you did. And no, I will not help you." Rachel laughed as Amy groaned in displeasure.

"I think it will be great having a new teacher on board. Weren't you tired of ol' Mrs. Anderson?"

"Yes, but this late in the summer? School starts next week!" Amy hefted the bags onto the granite countertop and began fishing within the paper bag to pull out groceries. She walked a carton of orange juice over to the refrigerator and began reorganizing the shelves to make room for the new products.

"Another bonus I hear is that he is gorgeous," Rachel continued.

Amy popped her head out of the fridge to look at her friend. Rachel wriggled her eyebrows playfully and tossed Amy a bag of cheese.

"Not you too," Amy sighed. "You and your hormones," Amy muttered just loudly enough for Rachel to hear.

Laughing, Rachel stacked the loaves of hamburger buns on the bar and began unpacking the fruit. "Not for me!"

Amy poked her head out of the refrigerator again. "No. Don't even think about trying to play matchmaker between this newbie and me. I do not want to deal with that on top of showing him the ropes."

"Come on, Ames!" Rachel teased. "Gorgeous new man teaching across the hall from you who doesn't know anyone else and needs a friend. A good friend…"

"Then we will make sure that he and Aaron are not only neighbors but also *good* friends," Amy stated with a huff of frustration.

"Did I hear my name?" Aaron called as they heard the sliding back door closing and his feet shuffling across the floor.

"In here!" Amy called.

He emerged in the doorway of the kitchen and watched as both women were preoccupied with stowing groceries. He motioned for Cade to take a seat at the island. "What's the current topic of conversation?"

"Oh, Rachel is making a fuss over the new teacher and trying to play matchmaker," Amy explained from the refrigerator. He heard a drawer close. "She thinks you two should be best friends."

"I did not say that!" Rachel called from the pantry, walking out and then stopping once her gaze fell on Aaron and the new teacher. She blushed and then looked at Amy's back and realized her friend had not noticed they had extra company either. She smirked at Aaron.

"Making a fuss?" Aaron asked curiously and winked at Cade.

"Oh, you know, rumor has it he is handsome, and hormones start flyin'." He saw Amy waving her hands as she spoke. "I guess that is a problem working with a bunch of women."

"Of which you are one, Ames."

He heard her grumble. "Yes, but I am not one of *those* women."

Laughing, Aaron accepted the glass of tea from Rachel and Cade nodded his thanks for his as well. How did he feel about being the topic of conversation? He wasn't sure, but he was intrigued by the woman whose head was currently stuck in the refrigerator.

"I hear his classroom will be across the hall from yours," Aaron baited.

"Don't remind me. I just found out about it a half hour ago."

"You don't sound too excited."

"I'm not."

"Why? I thought you would be happy to be rid of Mrs. Anderson."

"That's what I said!" Rachel chimed in.

"I am." Amy pushed another drawer into place and then started sorting through the top shelf.

"Then what is the problem?"

"For one, you never arrange your refrigerator. I mean some of this is just gross, Aaron. And second, it's not really a problem, it's just a new teacher. New teachers take time. Gotta show them the ropes, help them with lesson planning, help them interact with the students, blah, blah, blah."

"He's taught before," Aaron defended.

"Doesn't matter. New school, new way of doing things."

"You love helping people, Ames. I'm surprised you don't want to."

"I do love helping people. That's my problem. I'm behind on my own preparations right now, and we all know once I'm asked to help him, I'm going to put off my own stuff and push myself even further behind." Amy stepped from the fridge and closed the door. Turning toward Aaron, she froze. "Oh." She flashed a welcoming and genuine smile. "Hi there. I didn't realize Aaron had brought company." Her eyes met a warm brown gaze sheltered in a lean, tan face with defined jaw and a clean-cut hairstyle that looked like he came straight from the pages of Forbes. She extended her hand. "I'm Amy Frasier."

Cade reached across the counter and clasped her hand, a sudden awareness passing between them at the contact. He smiled. "Cade Wickerson. Nice to meet you."

"So how do you know this crazy dude?" She pointed at Aaron as she reached for a can of cashews, popped the lid and slid the canister to Aaron, who popped a few into his mouth but could not hide his smile.

"We will be working together," Cade replied and chuckled as shock, embarrassment, and frustration all crossed over her face. "I'm the new teacher."

CHAPTER TWO

Amy struggled to gather her thoughts, much less find her voice. She flushed. "Well, isn't that something, Rachel? The man of the hour is now in Aaron's kitchen."

Rachel offered a shy smile and shook his hand. "Rachel Cline, Chemistry teacher."

"Cade Wickerson, English and Literature." He smiled at her, and a blush crawled up Rachel's neck and to her cheeks.

"Welcome to the team," she greeted, pulling her hand away from his. Amy popped a cashew in her mouth and leaned on the counter across from him.

"So, you will be across the hall from me, Mr. Wickerson."

"So I hear." His lips quirked into a half grin and had her pulse kicking up a notch. The man was gorgeous *and* friendly, she thought. "I promise not to bug you with too many questions."

Ouch, she thought. She waved him away. "No, I don't mind helping you out if you need it. As much as I complain about Mrs. Anderson, your predecessor, I fear I'm well on my way to becoming much like her. She would be all grumbly and out of sorts right about now as well, so I need to nip that in the bud and get happy. I am happy you are taking her place. She should have retired years ago. You will be a breath of fresh air on the West Wing."

"West Wing?" he asked curiously.

"Our wing of the building. Lucky for you, you will be teaching on the cool side of the building."

"Whatever!" Aaron and Rachel yelled at the same time.

Cade chuckled. "Is it a competition?"

"Everything with Amy is a competition," Rachel stated with an eye roll.

Cade flashed a charming grin and leaned forward, snatching the cashew out of Amy's fingers before she could pop it into her mouth. She looked at him in surprise. "Well, it's a good thing I'm competitive then." He winked at her and popped the nut in his mouth.

Amy felt her face brighten and she turned to grab a glass out of the cabinet. Aaron and Rachel exchanged grins, knowing their friend was flustered by Cade.

"What are you really doing in here, Aaron?" Amy poured herself a glass of tea and waltzed back over to the counter. Reaching for the cashews, she paused and cast Cade a suspicious glance. When he did not advance, she grabbed a nut and popped it into her mouth. He grinned. The woman was feisty, and he liked that. He also liked the way her right brow rose when she was intrigued or surprised. That sexy brow, combined with her hazel eyes and sleek cheek bones created a stunning face. Her chestnut hair only added to the exquisite picture and made him want to know her more.

"Well, Ames, it is my house. That aside, Cade walked over from next door, so I thought I would introduce you to the new teacher."

"Are you sure you want to be his neighbor?" Amy asked Cade, pointing at Aaron. "It sort of comes with strings attached." She pointed to herself and Rachel.

"That is the truth," Aaron agreed, but with a warm grin so as to take away the sting.

"I think it will be a good move for me," Cade said.

Amy tilted her head and studied him closely. "Then it's settled. I will be your friend."

"You will?" Cade placed a hand on his heart and then swiped his brow. "Man, that was a close call. I've never had to work so hard for a friendship in my entire life. I also didn't realize you lived here too."

Amy struggled not to smile but lost the battle. She liked Cade. He seemed laidback, kind, and funny; all perks when added to his great looks. "I don't. I live a couple of blocks over. Rachel and I are just here all the time bugging the daylights out of Aaron. It's our civic duty."

Cade's cell phone rang. He glanced at the caller id. "Ah, I must take this. Be right back."

He stepped into the living room and answered. "I'm next door at the moment. I'll step out on the porch now." He hung up and popped his head back into the kitchen. "Just have to step out here to grab R."

Aaron nodded. When the door closed behind him, Amy swatted Rachel with a hand towel and her friend gasped. "Why didn't you tell me he was in the room?"

Rachel laughed. "And avoid that awkward introduction? No way."

"Jerk," Amy muttered on a smirk.

"He's handsome though, right?" Rachel nudged Amy with her elbow and Amy just shook her head in dismay.

"Easy, girl," Amy teased.

Rachel clapped her hands. "I'm going to run to the guestroom and change into my party clothes. She grabbed her duffle. "You two going to be okay out here? No buffer needed?"

"We're fine," Aaron chuckled as Rachel darted down the hall and closed the door.

"In all seriousness, Cade seems like a nice guy." Amy sliced up several oranges and popped them into a drink decanter. "I'm glad you will have a decent neighbor now and I will enjoy not seeing Mrs. Anderson pick her nose anymore."

Aaron laughed and cringed. "Oh, Mrs. Anderson. P.S. 14 will be a lonely place without her judgmental stare."

"Speak for yourself," Amy replied. "You know what it's been like across the hall from her the last three years? Man..." Amy shook her head but couldn't help the laugh that bubbled forth. "It will be nice for a change this year." She looked up as Cade walked back into the house followed by a lanky teenager that was the spitting image of him. Her hands froze in her slicing as she surveyed the two of them next to one another. *Did he have a son?* Aaron had left out that information. The boy's gaze travelled appreciatively over Amy before his eyes met hers and he blushed, looking away.

"Could I get some water?" the boy asked.

"Sure thing." Aaron pointed to the refrigerator and the kid walked behind the counter and helped himself. Amy followed him with her gaze and then looked back to Cade, who seemed not to notice.

The boy turned to leave. "Hey, kid," Amy called, causing the teen to turn around. She extended her hand. "I'm Amy."

"Rilan." He shook her hand with a shy smile.

"You're a tall one. How old are you?" Amy asked with a flick of her hand to a bar stool.

Aaron and Cade chuckled as the kid slid next to Cade at the bar. Cade lightly slapped him on the back before turning back to his own cup.

"Sixteen." His voice alternated between the deepening tones of manhood and the higher notes of childhood.

"You all unpacked?" Cade asked.

"Yes sir," Rilan replied, taking a sip of his water and shyly looking around.

"Remember, at around six, you need to stay at the house. It will be rather crowded out front with all the cars parking, but it is definitely not a party for you, so I want you to stay at the house. No going anywhere," Cade explained.

"Yes sir. I was going to test out my new video game."

"Good deal."

"That sucks," Amy responded, catching a warning look from Aaron. She shrugged. "I'll bring you a plate of delicious food later. At least you can enjoy some aspect of the party."

"That'd be awesome." Rilan's face lit up but Cade waved his hand. "No need. Thank you, Amy, but there's plenty of food at the house. He can just whip up a sandwich."

The boy sank in his seat and slid off quietly. "Thanks for the water," he mumbled, before dragging his feet toward the exit. The quiet click of the front door was the only indication of his departure.

"He seems like a nice kid."

Cade looked up at Amy and nodded. "Thanks. He is."

Amy's mind filled with questions. *How old were you when you had him? Where is his mother?* She wanted to ask away but knew her questions would need to be filtered over the course of a few hours, if not days. She just met the man; she didn't want to bombard him with twenty questions.

"He looks just like you." This caused a smile she was not expecting after his harsh reprimand to the kid.
"Don't tell him that."

Amy smiled in return and sighed. "Alright." She wiped her hands on a towel and then exited the kitchen. "It is 5:45 and I just saw Suzanne pull in. Of course, she is early. And I'm sure Rosa is not far behind her, then Eric. So... I am going to change right quick." She walked down the hall toward the guest bedroom and slipped inside.

"You ready to meet everyone?" Aaron asked with a playful smile as a knock sounded on the door.

"I guess so." Cade wiped his hands off and stood as well, walking toward the cooler and grabbing a soda as Aaron opened the door to the first guests.

∞

Amy circled from group to group, talking and planning with several of her teacher friends. Rachel waved her down and walked over to her. "So... Cade?" She beamed. "Aaron said you two seemed to hit it off earlier."

Amy looked at her in surprise. "Hit it off? If he means we were we able to hold a conversation, then yes, I guess we did."

Rachel rolled her eyes. "Come on, I was just asking for details." She bobbed her black hair and her sapphire eyes sparkled. "He seems nice, though."

"He is, from what I gather."

"Look, Suzanne is all but hanging all over the poor guy. Maybe you could be a friend and help him out."

"Why me?" Amy asked curiously, as she popped a potato chip in her mouth.

"Because you're good at stuff like that, Ames. You're friendly and nonthreatening, funny and sarcastic. Guys like that about you. It makes you easy to talk to," Rachel explained softly, her gaze following Aaron as he walked over to the grill to check the burgers.

"I see. Stop checking out Aaron."

Rachel nearly spit out her sip of tea, the action causing her to cough uncontrollably. "I was not!" She took a deep breath as her red face tightened before another deep cough.

Amy slapped her on the back several times and laughed before walking into the house. She grabbed a plate and worked her way through the bar. No one was in the house but her, and she realized she hadn't followed through on her food delivery next door. She then made her way back outside to the grill and grabbed a hot dog and a hamburger from Aaron.

"Hungry?" Aaron teased as he eyed her plate.

"I'm fixing it for the kid," she replied as she placed a piece of cheese on the burger and filled the plate with chips and dips.

"Thought Cade already saw to that."

"Kid deserves more than a sandwich when we are over here partying. Plus, I don't think Suzanne will let Cade get away long enough for him to even check on Rilan."

Aaron laughed. "True. She has had her claws in him most of the evening, hasn't she? The poor guy. He's too nice."

Amy finished preparing the plate and raised her soda toward Aaron. "I'll be back."

She walked through the house and outside and headed toward the brick house next door and knocked. A few seconds went by, and the door swung open. Rilan smiled shyly.

"Hey, kid," Amy greeted warmly. "You hungry? I wasn't sure if Cade was serious about the whole sandwich thing or if he planned to bring you food, but he's been kind of tied up meeting everyone."

The kid shook his head and accepted the plate, his eyes widening at the amount of food.

"I wasn't sure if you would like a hamburger or hot dog, or which dip, or all of it. So yeah... you got all of it," Amy confessed as her eyes roamed around the room. Her gaze fell upon the television, and she grinned. "Is that the new zombie apocalypse game?"

He grinned as she passed by him and walked over to the television stand, grabbing the case and reading the back of it. "It is!" she stated excitedly. "This is awesome."

Rilan eased on the edge of the couch and took a bite of his burger. He handed her the game control. "You can play if you want."

"Oh, I don't play."

Confusion fluttered over his face as he studied her. "Then why are you so excited about it?"

"Because I like to watch others play it." Amy sat on the couch as well and continued looking through the game information pages.

"Why?"

She looked at him as if he were the one confused. "Because it's zombies. It's like watching a creepy movie, only you get to help the people keep an eye out. I used to watch Aaron play all the time."

He grinned. "I'm pretty good at it."

"Yeah?" She tilted her head as she cast him a scrutinizing gaze, making him think she didn't believe him. "Prove it."

He finished the last bite of his burger in one giant bite and snatched his remote, unpausing the game and playing with an intense expression.

Amy made grimacing noises as she watched zombie heads explode. She would call out when she spotted one coming for him, and he'd take it down in expert fashion. He wasn't lying; he was good. Time passed and she hadn't even realized she'd opted for a zombie video game over a work party. Instead, she cried out and pointed at the screen, Rilan taking down zombie threats one after another.

∞

Cade glanced around the party, already exhausted from trying to memorize faces, names, classroom numbers, and connections. One face he didn't see, though, was Amy's. She was missing from the crowd. Walking over to Aaron, he accepted the fresh glass of tea Aaron offered. "So, you know everyone's names yet?"

Cade laughed and shook his head. "Hardly. But I have learned, according to Suzanne, who I should speak to and who I should not speak to. Amy being on the 'do not speak to' list. She doesn't seem to care for Amy. Why is that?"

Aaron grunted. "Ah. That would be because Amy was asked out by the most eligible bachelor on the faculty, Coach Eric Stanton." Aaron pointed, soda in hand, to a man laughing amongst fellow teachers as he spoke.

"Oh, I see. And Suzanne liked the man?"

"All the female teachers do, except Amy. She turned him down, but the fact she was chosen immediately placed her on the women's hate list."

"That's a shame," Cade chuckled. "Where did she go?"

Aaron glanced around as if just now noticing her absence. "I don't know. She went to give Rilan a plate of food. She may still be over there."

Cade turned to Aaron with a surprised expression and then walked toward the house. He had forgotten about dinner for Rilan, though he had told him to just make a sandwich. But as he cut through the backyard fence to his back, sliding glass door, he heard Amy squeal.

"Agh! Creepy Music! Creepy Music! They're coming! Get'em!"

Cade stepped into the living room and had Amy hurtling off the couch in a scream of surprise. Rilan paused the game and laughed at her antics as well as the surprised face of Cade.

Amy blushed as she held a hand to her rapidly racing heart. "Geez, Wickerson. You scared me." She swiped away the stray hairs that flew into her face and then apologized. "Sorry for the scream, kid."

"No problem," Rilan answered with a cheerful smile.

"What are you doing in here?" Cade asked, his gaze travelling from her to Rilan.

"Oh, I brought Rilan some food earlier. He was showing me his new game. He's pretty good." She tousled the kid's hair affectionately as he attempted to keep playing.

Cade stood still in surprise. "Um... well thank you for thinking of him. Unfortunately, his game time is over, and he needs to finish his summer reading."

Amy caught the slight harshness in Cade's tone. Rilan quickly saved his game and turned it off, reaching for a thick book and carrying it over to a chair by the window. Amy stood awkwardly in the center of the room. She grabbed Rilan's empty plate and soda can. "See ya around, kid."

"Bye, Amy."

"Ms. Frasier," Cade corrected.

"Ms. Frasier," Rilan restated.

Amy flashed him a sympathetic smile and walked toward the back door, Cade following close behind her. "He's a good kid."

"Yes, he is." Cade followed her back into Aaron's house as she threw away the plate and soda can in the kitchen.

"Well, I guess I will see you sometime tomorrow. I'm heading out. Hope you were able to meet everyone." She grabbed her duffle bag and her purse, shuffling them both onto her shoulder.

"Wait, you're leaving?" Cade walked with her to the front door.

"Yes."

"Why?"

She shrugged her shoulders. "I don't hang out too much at these sorts of things. I say my hellos and then leave before the shooting barbs from other teachers penetrate my skin."

Baffled, Cade ran a hand through his hair. He had finally torn himself away from Suzanne long enough to chat with the woman he had wished to chat with all evening, and she was leaving. "Maybe you could stay a few more minutes?"

She tilted her head and her right eyebrow slightly rose in curiosity. "Possibly. Why?"

"Because I've just gotten a free moment to speak with you."

"Okay..."

She watched as he rubbed the back of his neck and deeply inhaled. "Ah..." His brain froze. He had no idea what he wanted to talk to Amy about. All he knew was that he wanted to talk to her and get to know her. How did he play this off as aloof?

The back door opened, and Aaron and Rachel walked inside. "Oh, hey guys," Aaron greeted.

"You leaving already, Ames?" Aaron tossed her another soda and she set it on the coffee table. "Yep, so I will not be needing one of those. The kid got me in the mood to watch zombies, so I'm going home, popping in a creepy flick, and doing some lesson plans. Man, I bet they will turn out awesome. Zombies and history... I can work with that."

"The kid?" Rachel asked curiously.

Amy motioned toward Cade with her thumb. "Yeah, Cade's kid. Oh, right. You were changing when he came over earlier. He's at their place next door."

Rachel's eyes widened slightly in surprise. "I didn't realize you had a son," Rachel commented. Before Cade could respond, Amy shouldered her duffle once again. "Yeah, he's a cool kid. We'll probably have him in our classes."

She walked toward the front door. "I'll come by tomorrow to help clean up." She slipped out the front door with a wave.

Aaron smirked at Cade's obvious disappointment at her departure.

"You must have been young when you had him, if he's old enough to take classes from us," Rachel commented.

Before Cade could reply, Suzanne walked into the house. "Oh, there you are, Mr. Wickerson."

Cade inwardly cringed, but his muttered "Oh brother" was heard by Aaron and Rachel, who tried to stifle their giggles at his trepidation.

CHAPTER THREE

The next morning, Amy sat at the top of the ladder in her classroom and painted the bold blue stripe around her walls. She dipped her brush into the paint can and lightly touched up the corner of the wall while listening to classical music. She loved the quiet of the classroom before students and class bells and deadlines flooded the school. The calm, the quiet, the hopes of a great new school year all lingered in the air and her blood pumped with excitement. She had heard the door across the hall open earlier but had yet to see Cade. She wondered if it was him that arrived or just maintenance checking the trashcans. She eagerly wanted to check, but she also did not want to bother him.

Who was she kidding? She definitely wanted to bother him. She shook her head. *No. No thoughts like that*, she thought. Yes, Cade was handsome and kind, and yes, he had a cool son, but that did not mean she needed to let her mind wander beyond the professional. She barely knew the man, and he was already the hottest topic in the teachers' lounge that morning. Amy shook her head in annoyance. She hoped Cade's transition into the school would not be a hard one due to the buzz around his looks and his arrival.

"Amy?" a voice called from the doorway. She glanced down and over and saw Rilan's head poke through her doorway. "Ms. Frasier," he corrected sheepishly before looking around the room. She smiled. "Hey, kid." He looked up and his eyes widened in surprise to see her perched on the top of the ladder. She waved and began to climb down.

"How are ya?" She stuffed her paint brush into the can and watched as he shrugged.

"Kind of bored."

"And school hasn't even started yet," Amy sighed. "Give it time. It will only get worse."

Rilan grinned at her response.

Cade stood in the doorway and watched the exchange between Rilan and Amy. She was warm and friendly to Rilan, and she seemed genuinely interested in his classes as he began rattling off about his schedule for the new year.

She looked up and spotted Cade. "Hey there, neighbor."

"Sorry for the interruption." He nodded toward Rilan.

"I'm not. I needed a break." She pointed to her painting project. "You paint those pink walls yet?" She nodded toward his classroom and Cade grimaced and rubbed a hand over the back of his neck. "Yeah, I was just figuring out a game plan for that."

"Good luck." She grinned mischievously. "It's going to be a beast."

Cade chuckled. "That it will be. I can't believe someone actually taught in there every day. I've been in there ten minutes and already have a headache."

Laughing, Amy pointed to her own classroom. "Now you see why I go with calming skies and shades of blue." He and Rilan both looked up at her ceiling, the realistic floating clouds against a blue sky made the room feel like it had a glass ceiling.

"You did this?" Cade asked, impressed by her skill.

She nodded. "One of the first things I did when I started teaching here a few years ago. My classroom doesn't have windows like yours does, and I felt too closed in. I needed air. So, I brought the outdoors in." She smiled.

"It's awesome," Rilan stated, causing Amy's smile to spread even wider.

"Glad you like it, though it's too bad you won't get to enjoy it. Saw on that schedule of yours just now that you have Mr. Royce for History instead of me. What's up with that?"

Rilan rolled his eyes and pointed his thumb at Cade. "This guy made me sign up for debate class, which overlaps with your class."

"Lame," Amy ribbed Cade with a wink.

"Totally," Rilan played along, as Cade waved his hands to ward off their teasing.

"You will thank me one day when you're at college and have to stand before your class and give a report, or when you take debate in college."

"I don't plan on taking debate in college," Rilan recited as though he'd made the same argument before.

Amy bit back a smile as she watched them battle it out. Cade caught her amused expression and sighed. "Fine."

Rilan's eyes widened in surprise. "What?"

"I said, fine. If you don't want to take debate, you can switch classes."

Rilan cheered and Cade spoke up to be heard over the excitement. "*But* you have to take another extracurricular to replace it."

"Deal." Rilan high-fived Cade. "You're the best, Uncle Cade." He rushed from the room, and they could hear his feet echoing up the hall as he headed towards the office, no doubt to see whether he could coerce the school counselor into changing his classes before the first day of school.

"Uncle? You're his uncle?" Amy asked. "I thought Rilan was your son." She smiled sheepishly. "I'm pretty sure everyone thinks that. You two look so much alike."

"Yeah, most people think that, but I would've had to be his age when he was born."

Amy tilted her head in consideration.

"Which I realize is still a possibility in some cases," Cade clarified. "But not for me. Rilan is my brother's son. *Was,*" he corrected. "Was my brother's son." His voice trailed off. "He passed away in a car accident about five years ago. And Rilan's mom two years prior to that. Cancer."

"I'm so sorry." Amy reached out and gently rested a hand on his arm. "It's wonderful that you two have one another though."

"Oh yeah. He's a good kid for the most part. Makes it pretty easy, even when life hasn't always been."

"Well, you certainly had me fooled. You two seem like two peas in a pod."

Cade smiled proudly. "Thanks." He held her gaze a moment longer and she diverted her eyes toward the door as a knock sounded on the doorframe. Coach Eric Stanton walked into the room. "Ah, Amy." He glanced briefly at Cade before turning his attention back to her. "Sorry to interrupt."

"No worries, Eric. What can I do for you?"

"Several of us are getting together on Friday night at Burgundy's Bar to celebrate the end of summer and to kick off the new year. I wanted to invite you to come out."

"Um, I don't know," Amy began, feeling awkward at receiving an invitation that Eric was purposely not extending to Cade.

"Think about it and let me know. We can ride together." Eric flicked a wave toward Cade as he walked back to the door, spotting Rilan as he squeezed by the coach and back into Amy's classroom. Eric studied the teenager a moment and then looked at Cade. He didn't ask, but the thought was written on his face as he continued to walk down the hall.

"Who was that guy?" Rilan asked.

"Coach Stanton," Amy told him. "He coaches the varsity girls' basketball team."

"Oh, good. He looked mean. Glad I don't have to worry about a class with him."

Cade hissed in disapproval at his nephew's candor and Rilan flushed. "I mean... I'm sure he's a nice man."

Amy grinned, and a laugh released before she could stop it and it only grew worse as Cade turned his disapproving glare on her instead of Rilan. She patted his arm. "Oh, come on. You can't tell me you don't think the same thing."

Slowly, Cade's stern façade faded away and he smirked. "Anyway..." He attempted to steer the conversation in a different direction and Amy pointed to her paint. "I need to finish wrapping up my work."

"Right." Cade cleared his throat and motioned for Rilan to head back across the hall. "We'll get out of your hair."

Amy paused, paintbrush in hand as she covered the paint can with its lid. "Would you guys want to go grab supper?"

Cade's brows lifted slightly at her invitation and Rilan eyed his uncle for a response.

"Um, that's a nice offer, Amy."

She tilted her head and her eyes squinted. "But..." She trailed off, waiting for his excuse.

Cade flushed. "No but. I just don't want to keep you from finishing your work here."

"I'm finished." She pointed to the completed blue stripe along her wall. "Hey, while we're at it, we can go by the hardware store and pick out some paint for your classroom. Unless you're planning on keeping the pink."

Cade studied her a moment and then nodded. "Alright. Sounds like a plan."

"Good. Let me wash this brush out and I'll head on over to your room in a few."

Cade nodded in agreement as he and Rilan headed toward the ostentatious room across the hall.

∞

Amy slid into the booth across from Rilan and Cade and popped a fry into her mouth. "So, what literature do you have picked out for your students so far?"

Cade sighed and lightly ran a hand over his cheek as if he were stressed about the topic at hand. "I have several, but I'm struggling with which particular ones I want to use for certain topics. I know I will have them read some Shakespeare." Amy made a face of disgust that made him laugh. "*But*," he continued. "I am also going to make them read some Chaucer."

"Now Chaucer is where it's at," Amy agreed.

"You're a fan of Chaucer?"

"Very much so. I like his attitude, his humor, his sarcasm. He is a literary genius." Amy's eyes lit up as she spoke. "He wrote one of my favorite works, Troilus and Criseyde."

"You prefer Troilus and Criseyde over Romeo and Juliet?" Cade asked, intrigued by her enthusiasm.

"Definitely. Now don't get me wrong, Shakespeare has some incredible works. Macbeth is pretty interesting. But Chaucer just has a way with words that speaks to me." Amy blushed at her outburst and took a bite of her fried chicken.

Cade studied her in silence for a moment. "I wholeheartedly agree with you. I'm a Chaucer fan as well." He watched as her eyes lit in amusement and then traveled to Rilan as he popped a French fry into his mouth and looked bored with their current topic of conversation.

"Are you falling asleep on us, kid?" she teased.

"Almost." Rilan accepted the light elbow jab from his uncle in good humor as a voice carried toward them.

 "Ms. Frasier? Mr. Wickerson? Is that you?" Amy inwardly cringed and forced a smile. "Hey, Suzanne."

Cade nodded in welcome as he watched Suzanne survey Rilan and her eyes bounced back and forth between the two of them. No doubt she was trying to figure out if he was Cade's son.

"You finish setting up your classroom?" Suzanne asked.

"I did today, actually, so, I'm officially ready for the school year. You?"

Suzanne waved her hot pink nails. "Oh, I finished up weeks ago. I've just been helping others prep the last few weeks."

"Well, that's kind of you." Amy's smile was polite, but Cade could sense an underlying tension between the two women.

"Speaking of classrooms—" Suzanne placed a hand on Cade's shoulder.

Rilan's eyes quickly flashed towards the woman standing next to his uncle, his eyes curious. "Did you need any help with your new space, Mr. Wickerson?"

Amy bit back a grin as she watched Cade's face blanch slightly at being put on the spot.

Rilan picked up on his uncle's awkwardness and draped his arm over Cade's shoulders. "That's okay, ma'am. He's got me."

Suzanne's blue eyes narrowed on Rilan a moment before she plastered a smile on her face. "Of course he does. Wonderful." She shifted her purse from one shoulder to the next. "Well, it was good seeing you again." She squeezed Cade's arm and shot Amy a narrowed gaze of disapproval as she walked away.

Rilan whistled under his breath. "Look out, Uncle Cade. I'm pretty sure that woman has her sights set on you."

Cade choked on his drink as Amy and Rilan snickered. Receiving a sympathetic pat on his back from his nephew, Cade just shook his head and avoided further discussion on the topic as he gathered his trash and walked it toward the garbage can.

"Who was that lady?" Rilan whispered to Amy while his uncle was away from the table.

"Suzanne Meters. Do yourself a favor. That extracurricular class you have to take—"

"Yeah?" Rilan asked.

"Just make sure it's not Home Ec." Amy's lips tilted into a smile as Rilan's jaw dropped at the knowledge that Suzanne was a fellow high school teacher he could potentially have in class.

"Thanks for the advice."

Amy winked as Cade walked back up to the table. "Ready?"

They slid from the booth and stood.

"Hardware store?" Amy asked.

"Only if you want to," Cade added.

"Sure." She reached in her purse for her keys. "Want to ride together?"

"Oh. Sure. Yeah, we could do that." Cade reached into his pocket for his keys.

"Mine or yours?" she asked.

"We can take mine." Cade held open the door as Amy and Rilan walked out of the restaurant and toward his waiting truck. He clicked the locks and seemed pleased to see his nephew's manners as he opened Amy's door for her. She slipped inside and Rilan shut it. "Can I drive?"

"Dream on." Cade shoved his shoulder as he passed by him.

"Uncle Cade," Rilan whined as he opened the back door and hopped inside. He waited until Cade was seated up front before continuing. "You're eventually going to have to let me drive. I have my license, you know?"

"Oh, is that so? How did I not remember that?" Cade replied with equal sarcasm.

Amy grinned at the banter between them.

"I aced my driver's test too."

"Yes, but that wasn't here in the city."

"This is the suburbs," Rilan corrected. "I think I can handle it."

"We'll see, but not today." Cade navigated his way toward the nearest hardware store and Amy tried not to study him too much. The man intrigued her. He was obviously an amazing uncle to Rilan; their unique relationship was sweet, and their camaraderie natural. No telling the tragedies they'd faced together over the years. She silently sent up a prayer of thanks that they had one another before a shriek sounded and Cade slammed on his brakes and swerved to avoid an accident in front of them.

CHAPTER FOUR

Cade gripped the wheel and his chest tightened at what could end up being a dangerous accident if he didn't somehow navigate his truck away from the destruction happening before him in the three-car pileup. He swerved and hopped the sidewalk, his truck scraping against a fire hydrant as he whipped his wheel to the side and tried to make the turn onto the side street instead of toward the intersection they were originally approaching. When he saw the other truck speed through the stoplight, the other two cars turning did not stand a chance. Various other cars swerved to avoid collision, then his truck spun in circles, and he felt Amy's grip on his arm as Rilan's scream from the back seat sounded through the car. Finally, his truck came to a stop and other than everyone's labored and panicked breathing, silence hung in the cab. He took a calming breath and then released the steering wheel. He turned and gripped Amy's hand. "You okay?" He turned a panicked look to the backseat. "Rilan?"

Rilan bent his head between his knees and muttered, "I'm okay."

Cade leaned his head back against the headrest and tried to still his haywire heart. Amy's hand still gripped his forearm. He wasn't sure she realized it because she sat frozen in place, her eyes wide, and face pale. Sirens sounded and slowly the scene beside them filled with emergency personnel and law enforcement. An officer ran to Cade's window.

He rolled it down.

"Everyone okay in your vehicle, sir?"

Cade nodded. "Just shaken up, officer."

"Sit tight for a few. If you think any of you need checked out, EMTs are available. Otherwise, please stay in your vehicle until we secure the crash site. We'll have questions."

"Yes sir." Cade rolled his window up again and then planted his face in his hands.

Amy's fingers slowly eased from his arm, and he felt her rub a soothing circle in the middle of his shoulder blades. He looked up. "I'm so sorry, Amy."

Her eyes glistened with unshed tears, mostly from shock, but her smile was a watery one that had him hugging her against him. He reached toward Rilan and all but drew him over the center console to hug him close as well. "So sorry. So sorry," he muttered.

Rilan pulled away. "You have nothing to be sorry for, Uncle Cade. You were smart. You saved us."

Amy nodded against his chest before easing back to look up at him. He felt her body still shaking, but she put on a brave face as she reached for Rilan's hand and squeezed it for reassurance that he was also okay.

"Everyone is okay and that is what matters." She exhaled a deep breath of relief.

"I don't think I'm up for a trip to the hardware store now, though," Rilan confessed.

Cade and Amy both nodded.

"We'll just wait for clearance and then we'll head home. Shouldn't be too long since we weren't in the main mix up," Cade assured him. An officer walked up to Cade's truck and signaled for him to step out. He unbuckled his seat belt and exited, shutting his door.

"That was close." Rilan released a deep breath and Amy turned in her seat to face him.

"Yes, it was. But your uncle was smart."

"I guess he told you my dad died in a car accident?"

"He did," she admitted. "You okay?"

Rilan nodded, though he swallowed back tears. "Just scares me, ya know?"

Amy nodded in understanding. "I imagine your uncle is feeling the weight of that right now as well."

"Yeah, I'm sure he is. I think it's one reason he doesn't want me driving on my own yet. Which, right now, I'm thankful it was him behind the wheel this time instead of me."

She patted his knee as Cade opened the door and handed Amy a clipboard. She read over the paper and signed her name and filled out her personal information. Cade handed it back to the police officer and then slid into the driver's seat. "We are free to go." Cade buckled his seat belt. The smell of rubber still permeated the air, and he knew he'd worn his tires down a bit in the spins, but they'd all held and didn't blow. For that, he was grateful.

"Can you just take me home?" Amy asked.

Cade turned. "What about your car?"

"I'll have Aaron pick it up." She avoided his gaze a moment. "I'm not really wanting to drive right now."

"I understand." Cade blew a frustrated breath. "I'm so sorry about this, Amy."

He saw the regret on her face before she spoke. "I didn't mean to make you feel bad. I don't blame you for this. You were fantastic. I'm just a bit jittery."

Somewhat reassured, Cade nodded. "Where do I go?"

"Like you're headed to your house. I only live a couple of blocks over."

"Oh, that's right."

The drive wasn't far considering they lived in one of the closest neighborhoods to the school, and as Amy directed Cade to her driveway, he regretted that their first real interaction outside of the classroom had to end on such a sour note.

When he parked, she unbuckled and grabbed her purse. "You boys get a good night's rest." She eyed Rilan a moment longer and the boy nodded.

Cade hopped out of the truck and waited at the hood of cab. "I'll walk you."

"Thanks." Amy's house was smaller than his and Aaron's, but it was a cute stone and brick combination that had a bright blue front door framed by potted plants of various bright colored flowers. She had a small sign in her yard cheering for the Bulldogs, their school mascot. She started to unlock her front door, but her hands shook, and the key slightly missed the keyhole. Cade reached forward and grasped her hand and gently took the keys from her. He then slipped it into the lock and turned it.

"Thanks," she whispered as she opened the door and was greeted by the familiar scents of home.

"Thanks for palling around with us a bit today. I'm sorry, again, about how the day ended up."

She offered an apologetic smile. "Don't be. Just get some rest and try to relax." Cade rubbed a hand over his face and sighed.

"Yeah. I'll try."

She squeezed his arm. "See you tomorrow."

He took a step back so she could close the door and made his way back to his truck. When he hopped inside, Rilan had already moved to the front passenger seat. "I like her," his nephew boldly stated.

Cade backed out of Amy's driveway and headed toward their own house.

"But I'm not sure we kicked this friendship off on the best foot," Rilan continued.

Cade released a grunt of agreement.

"You'll just have to step it up."

Cade turned to his nephew with a quizzical expression. "What are you talking about?"

Rilan grinned as he leaned his head back against the headrest and shut his eyes. "If you want to make it up to her, you'll have to step up your game."

"I think things will be just fine how they are."

"If you say so," Rilan mumbled. "But I like her, and I can tell you do too."

"She's a coworker."

"And really pretty."

"Easy, Tiger."

Rilan opened his eyes and skeptically looked at his uncle.

Cade's lips twitched. "I'm glad you think Amy's fun to be around—"

"And pretty," Rilan reminded him.

"And pretty," Cade acquiesced. "But I'm new to this school and city. It's going to take some time before I even think about dating someone."

"Oh, so you *were* thinking she's the dateable type?" Rilan teased.

"Alright," Cade chuckled. "That's enough."

Rilan held up his hands in surrender.

"When we get home, I want you to finish your summer reading chapters for the night, that way we can spend the evening just chilling after what happened today."

"Sounds good to me." He saw the worry in his uncle's face and gave a heartening slap on the shoulder. "You did good, Uncle Cade. You kept us safe."

His uncle's jaw tightened, and Rilan saw the tears sting the back of Cade's eyes as they pulled into their garage. He hopped out to give his uncle a minute to himself. And Cade was grateful for that calming minute. How close it had been. And Amy... His heart twisted at the thought of her and Rilan in harm's way. Thanking the heavens above for the added protection, Cade headed into the house on the inward promise that he was going to force himself to relax.

∞

Amy awoke with a groan, her head pounding, and vision speckled. A migraine. *Really? Three days before school was to start?* She eased to her feet and walked to her bathroom and ran a washcloth under the cool water. She then walked back to her bed and placed it over her forehead and threw the covers over her face.

She heard a light knock on her front door. Easing to her feet and walking down the hallway, she grabbed her sunglasses and slipped them on. The slight darkness blocked some of the painful light. She opened the door and mustered a small smile as Cade stood on her doorstep.

"Um... hello, Amy." Cade eyed her warily. "Are you feeling alright? You look a bit green."

Amy attempted a smile before nausea churned her stomach and she slapped a hand over her mouth.

She ran as she gagged and made it to the hallway bathroom in just enough time to hurl into the toilet.

Cade grimaced as he stepped inside the house, inviting himself in.

Cade walked down the hallway and into the restroom, where Amy sat on the floor, leaning against the cool tiled wall. Cade reached a hand toward her forehead. "You are burning up, Amy."

Amy turned her head from his touch and swatted his hand away, her lack of strength worrying him. He helped her to her feet, and she swooned. He caught her against his chest before she crashed into the wall. "Sorry about that," she whispered. "I have a massive migraine and I'm— not well." She gently nudged herself free of him and slowly made her way to the living room. She flopped onto the couch and held the cool washcloth to her forehead, eyes closed.

Cade sat on the edge of her coffee table and studied her. "Is there anything I can get you?"

She groaned.

"How can I help you, Amy?" he asked. "While I'm here, I might as well tend to what you need. If there is anything you need."

"I cannot really see you at the moment because my vision is so speckled."

"Do I need to call a doctor?"

"No," she muttered. "It will pass."

"Is this from yesterday? Did you hit your head during the accident?"

"No and no." A small smile tugged the corner of her mouth. "Stop worrying. This is actually a pretty normal occurrence. It's probably just from stress."

"Triggered by the anxiety of the car accident too, I'm sure." Cade heaved a sigh. "Do you have some medicine?"

"Already taken some. It's really just a waiting game right now." She covered a hand over her towel-covered forehead.

Cade stood and walked toward what looked to be her kitchen. Amy could hear the sounds of her refrigerator ice maker and water dispenser, and he returned, setting a glass of ice water on a coaster.

"Thanks," she grumbled, one eye opening and peeking up at him. "What are you doing here anyway?"

"Checking up on you. Which I'm glad I did." Cade ran a hand over the back of his neck. "I think we should get you checked out by a doctor. What if it's whiplash from the spinning?"

"It's not."

"It could be." He placed his hands on his hips and she sighed, easing into a sitting position despite his protests.

"Cade, I appreciate you coming over and your concern, but I am fine. I suffer from migraines periodically. Have since junior high. I toss back a couple of migraine pills, drink ice water or a cold lemon lime soda, eat a few crackers, and wait it out. They usually only last a day or two."

"But school starts in a few days."

"And I'll be there."

"Well, if I can't help you here, and you won't let me take you to the doctor, is there anything I can do to help you up at the school?"

"Nope. I'm all set." He eased back onto the coffee table, and he heard her softly snicker. "You just don't know what to do with yourself now, hm?"

"Unfortunately, I have plenty that needs done, I just don't know how to leave you when you're laid up."

"That's sweet." She reached over and patted his hand. "But the best thing you could do for me is to leave. I just need peace and quiet and the dark."

"Okay, if you think that's it, I will get out of your hair. If you do need something, just let me know. I'm just a couple of streets over, I can be here in a minute if you need to go to the doctor. Here." He walked toward her entry table where a notepad and pen sat by the telephone. He jotted down his phone number and brought it to her. "Don't hesitate to call if you need something." When she didn't raise her arm to accept the paper, he placed it on the coffee table. He reached above her and grabbed the throw that rested over the back of the couch and spread it over her. "Take care, Amy."

"Thanks, Cade. I'll see you in a few days."

"Unless you need me," he corrected.

"Unless I need you," Amy repeated on a sigh as her eyes drifted closed once again. When she opened them a few minutes later, he was gone.

It was sweet of him to stop by to check on her, especially after what they'd gone through the day before. It was not exactly the smoothest introduction to someone new. He seemed like a nice guy, but Amy had a hard time with friendships. Especially the new ones. And several of the teachers already despised her due to Eric Stanton pursuing her the last couple of years. For the next most available bachelor to even show kindness toward her might make her permanently blacklisted. She groaned as she remembered Eric's invite for the evening. Surely he wouldn't come to pick her up without her officially saying yes to his invitation, but she wouldn't put it past him. Groaning, she sort of wished she'd taken Cade up on the doctor offer. At least then she might avoid Eric by not being home. She felt bad for the thought, but as pain pierced through her temple, she let herself drift into a deep sleep.

CHAPTER FIVE

Cade dragged the paint roller down the wall of his classroom as Rilan and a maintenance man named Rodney helped along the other wall. He'd gone with a standard cream color. He'd have to come up with something more creative later, but for now it had to work. School started in three days, so time was of the essence to get the flamingo pink room taken care of. Rodney had supplied him with an ample amount of air fresheners as well, and there was now only a faint trace of moth balls that lingered.

"Looks good in here." Aaron leaned against the door frame and watched as everyone continued painting.

"We're on the homestretch, I believe."

"Looks like it." Aaron tossed his thumb over his shoulder. "You seen Amy today?"

Cade set his roller down and walked over to him. "I went by her place earlier this morning. She has a migraine."

Aaron cringed. "Yikes. And you survived? I'm surprised she didn't cut you down in pieces and toss you out the back door."

"No. She seemed at ease, just in pain. I was checking on her."

"Checking on her? Why?" Aaron crossed his arms as he relaxed against the door.

"She didn't tell you?" Cade asked.

Aaron shook his head. "What happened to her?"

"We were in a small accident yesterday. Car accident."

Aaron jolted, back straight. "What? Is she okay? Are you okay?"

"We are fine." He pointed to himself and Rilan. "Amy says the migraine has nothing to do with it, but—"

"She gets them all the time," Aaron interrupted. "But man, an accident? Where?"

Cade reported exactly what took place the afternoon before and Aaron stood, mouth agape, at the retelling. "Wow." He shook his head in disbelief. "So glad you are all okay. Sounds like a close one."

"Yeah..." Cade fisted his hands in his pockets. "She probably won't ever want to ride with me again."

"I doubt that," Aaron smirked. "When Ames and I were in college, I crashed my truck into the side of the parking garage on campus. She was with me. Though she never let me live it down, she still rides with me every now and then."

"That's good to hear. Man, I feel terrible."

"Hey, look on the bright side. You guys had a fun afternoon and seem to be getting along." Travis motioned toward Amy's classroom again. "And that means you guys will be good hall buddies for the year."

"True. At least I hope so."

"It'll be great." Aaron shot him a thumbs up. "Listen, the last night before school starts, Rachel, Amy, and I always get together to have one last hoorah. Pizza and beer. Because that's what mature grownups do, right?" he joked. "You should come."

"Count me in." Cade shook Aaron's hand in thanks.

"Good deal. Well, I will let you get back to your cotton candy room."

Cade laughed. "Not much longer."

Aaron squinted. "I swear, even the walls that are already painted cream, it's like they still have a pink tint to them. I think my eyes are just so burned they can't adjust."

Cade laughed. "They better not be any shade of pink. I think I've had enough of it myself."

"Good luck with that. See ya Sunday."

"See ya." Cade walked back over to his paint roller and made sure he took an extra swish across the wall he'd just painted just to make sure all traces of pink were eradicated. But when he started looking around the room, he too felt jaded, and only saw more dreaded pink.

∞

Amy stepped out of the shower and wrapped her towel around her body and grimaced when she saw the bags under her eyes. Her migraine had finally faded into a dull, yet manageable ache. She rubbed her hand over the foggy mirror and erased enough steam to apply her face cream and twist her damp hair into a messy bun on top of her head. Opening the door, condensation followed her, and fog seeped into the hallway as she walked toward the kitchen.

"Ames!" Rachel shrieked, as Amy stepped into the living room.

She turned in enough time to see Aaron sitting on the couch. Amy gaped at her two friends. "What are you two doing here?"

"Cade told Aaron about the car accident. We came to check on you. When you didn't open the door, I freaked out and used my key." Rachel held up the key Amy had given her a few years prior.

"I'll be back in a second." She turned and walked back down the hallway.

Amy appeared at the edge of the hallway once more, now sporting a pair of yoga pants and a tank top and looking more refreshed than she'd felt for the last several hours. "You good to go for school in a couple days?" Aaron asked.

"I'll be right as rain," she smiled. "It's just a hint of a headache now, so I should be clear by tomorrow."

"You still coming by the house on Sunday for our traditional last supper of summer?"

"I'll be there with bells on. Well, maybe not bells." She tapped her sore temple. "But I will be there."

"Good. I invited Cade over as well. Figured it'd be nice for us to get to know him some more."

"He came and checked on me this morning. Thought that was sweet, though I feel he thinks it is partially his fault."

"He seemed pretty torn up over the car accident," Aaron admitted.

"It wasn't even that much of an accident on our end. I mean, yes, it was terrifying. But he handled it like a professional racecar driver, the way he swerved onto the side street. The truck went into a spin, and he seemed to anticipate its every move."

The doorbell rang and Amy groaned.

"I thought your head felt better." Rachel eyed her in concern.

"It's not my head. It's Eric."

"Ohhh." Rachel grinned. "The bar night?"

"Yes. He asked me to go. I never told him yes, mind you. But I have a feeling that is him here to pick me up for a night out on the town."

"Always persistent." Rachel giggled as the doorbell rang again.

Amy sent a pleading look to Aaron. He stood and walked over and opened the door. Surprise lit Eric's face. "Aaron?"

"Hey Eric, come on in." He waved him inside and shut the door, Eric's eyes found Amy perched on the arm of her sofa.

"Amy, I thought you'd be dressed by now." He glanced at his watch.

"I'm not going, Eric."

He stared for a moment. "Well, you could have called me."

"I never agreed to go in the first place." Amy's hackles rose, and Rachel placed a restraining hand on her arm.

"What Amy means, Eric, is that she's had a pretty rough couple of days. She was in a car accident yesterday and had a migraine today."

Concern etched Eric's face. "Oh my, are you okay?" he asked, stepping toward her.

She held up a hand and nodded. "Just a bit sore." Which wasn't a lie, she realized, as she rotated her shoulders to loosen her stiff muscles. The tension from her migraine must have partnered up with her tense muscles from the accident and decided to have a chess match.

"Well, I completely understand, Amy. Maybe another night." Eric looked to her with hopeful eyes.

"Maybe. Have fun, Eric." She waved to signal his departure, and he took the silent cue. He said his goodbyes to Aaron and Rachel as he disappointedly made his way to his car.

"Poor guy. You can't give him a little hope, Ames?" Aaron chuckled.

"No. Because Eric abuses a little encouragement into more than it is."

"That is true," Rachel pointed out. "I noticed that last year when he had eyes for Miranda Meeks."

Aaron shook his head. "Sometimes I forget we teach high schoolers and aren't in high school ourselves."

"It is what it is," Amy smirked as she headed towards the kitchen to fetch a glass of water. "So has Cade painted his room yet?"

"He was painting it this morning when I saw him. Rodney and Rilan were helping him."

"Oh good. I was hoping someone from maintenance would help him out. That room is a beast."

"*Was* a beast," Aaron corrected. "Looked like they would finish it up today."

Impressed, Amy's brows rose. "Way to go, Wickerson. I'm glad he's being proactive. Most newbies are scared to make changes to anything."

"True," Rachel said. "So maybe he won't be so burdensome after all." She winked, and Amy rolled her eyes.

"Just give up the matchmaking, Rachel."

"That's like asking grass not to grow," Aaron replied, accepting the punch to his shoulder from an embarrassed Rachel.

Amy laughed. "True."

"I just find it interesting that you were riding in his truck with him and his nephew yesterday," Rachel prodded. "You obviously like him enough to spend more time with him."

"He's a decent guy. Rilan seems like a great kid. I was going to help him pick out a paint color for his room, but we never made it to the hardware store."

"Still can't believe you guys were in an accident. It gives me chills." Rachel shuddered. "And because of that, I will let my interrogation and my goading rest for now."

"Thank you." Amy nodded with a relieved smile. "So, what are you two up to now that you've checked on me?"

"Well, I need to run to the store before calling it a night." Rachel stood and grabbed her wallet and keys.

"And I am headed over to Cade's for a bit to help him put together some of his furniture. Mainly bedframes."

"Well, tell him I said hello. I am going to go crawl back into bed and sleep the last of this headache away."

Rachel gave her a comforting hug. "Hope it works."

"Me too." Amy waved from her front porch as her two friends departed in separate vehicles, headed in opposite directions. She loved Aaron and Rachel. She'd often wished for them to fall in love with one another, but it wasn't in the cards. They were all too close to one another; neither could see the other as more than a friend. Though she had caught Rachel casting longer glances in Aaron's direction as of late, even if those didn't lead to more, that was okay too, Amy thought. Because friendship was the foundation to everything, not just relationships. And she liked that they could all get together and have an easy time together and value one another's company. She wondered how Cade would soon fit into the mix, but she also had to admit that part of her hoped he wouldn't always be just a friend. Which was absurd to even think about. She *just* met him, *and* she worked with him. She'd be a fool to date someone from work. But still, she thought of his concerned gaze from earlier that morning and a softness touched her heart. "Should be an interesting school year," she muttered to herself as she shuffled down the hallway to bed.

CHAPTER SIX

"Pizza's here!" Aaron called through his house as Rachel and Amy began walking into the living room. Aaron opened the door and Cade stood there. "Nevermind!" he called, not realizing the women had already walked inside the house. "Oh." Aaron smiled sheepishly as he saw Amy flinch from being so close when he yelled. "Come on in." He waved Cade inside. "Rilan not with you?"

Cade shook his head. "I wasn't sure if—"

"Of course, he can come," Rachel invited.

Smiling appreciatively, Cade thanked her. "I think he was pretty stoked to just play video games all night. Last night before school starts, or last night of freedom, as he likes to say."

"Can't blame him," Amy interjected. "Aren't we doing pretty much the equivalent?"

She walked up to Cade and slipped her arms around his waist and gave him a friendly hug of welcome. Aaron and Rachel watched in equal surprise as Cade at the gesture. "How are you feeling?" Amy looked up at him and asked.

"Better. You?" Her hazel eyes were free from pain, and he took that as a positive sign.

"Much better. Migraine free. Thanks again for checking on me."

"No problem."

"Did you get your room painted?"

"Yes. It's a bit blah right now, but I figure I can work on it in stages. It is, however, no longer pink."

"And that is a great start," Amy chuckled as she released him and walked toward the front door, opening it as the pizza delivery boy cleared the porch steps. "Saw him coming through the window." She grinned as the young boy smiled in greeting.

"What's up, Ms. Frazzle?"

"Hey Ryan! Oh, you know, just enjoying our last night student free." She winked at him as he handed her the two large pizzas. He waved over her shoulder. "Hey Mr. Jacobs!" Ryan stepped forward and high-fived Aaron. The boy's face flushed a touch when he saw Rachel. "Ms. Cline." Rachel waved.

"You ready for classes to start?" Aaron asked him.

"Oh yeah. I just received my schedule Friday."

"And?" Amy asked.

"And I am in all of your classes." His grin widened into an excited smile. "I don't know how I nailed that, but I'm glad. My brother loved having you all."

"Well, we look forward to seeing you tomorrow. Hopefully you still have that smile on your face at the end of the year," Amy teased. "Who do you have for English class? Do you remember?"

The boy's face fell. "Not Mrs. Bridges, which is good, but I don't know the teacher, so I'm not sure what to expect."

"Name?" Amy asked.

"A Mr. Wickerson," Ryan explained.

Amy grinned and motioned for Cade to step forward. "Meet Mr. Wickerson."

Ryan's face split into a friendly smile. "So he's your friend?" He looked to all of them for confirmation and they nodded. "Awesome." Somewhat relieved by that knowledge, Ryan extended his hand and Cade shook it. "Nice to meet you, sir. Ryan Carding."

"Nice to meet you, Ryan."

Ryan headed back toward the door. "I better get on. I've got another delivery to hit before 7:30 or they get it free."

Amy paid him and gave him a generous tip. "See you tomorrow, Ryan. Get a good night's rest."

"Yes, ma'am. See ya, Ms. Frazzle."

Amy shut the door.

"Ms. Frazzle?" Cade asked.

Amy blushed. "Just a nickname."

His brows rose as if he waited for her to explain.

"You know The Magic School Bus books?"

"I vaguely remember those."

"Ms. Frizzle is the teacher."

"Right…"

"Well, for some reason the students like to take Frasier and turn it into Frazzle."

"Because she's eccentric like Ms. Frizzle," Aaron continued.

"I'm not eccentric," Amy defended and then shrunk back a bit at Aaron's knowing gaze. "Okay, maybe I can be," she laughed.

"Nicknames usually mean you're well liked." Cade smiled at her.

"Or hated. Depends on the nickname."

"And what about you two? Nicknames?"

"Mr. J for me." Aaron rolled his eyes. "Because Jacobs is so hard to say," he laughed.

"And what about you, Rachel?" Cade asked.

Rachel's cheeks blushed. "No."

"Liar." Amy burst into laughter. "Rachel's nickname isn't exactly the same as ours."

"Why is that?"

"It's not one the students call her to her face." Aaron and Amy snickered as Rachel walked over to the pizza boxes and grabbed a slice. "Laugh it up, guys. Laugh it up," she muttered.

"Fine Cline isn't exactly appropriate for the students to shout out in the halls." Aaron nudged Rachel playfully as she swatted his hand.

Cade laughed. "I see."

"Don't worry, you'll get a nickname too. It will more than likely happen the first week of school, so better make a good impression." Amy winked at him as she bit into her own slice of pizza.

"I'm sure I will. Let's just hope it's a good one."

"Well at least you know one of your students. Ryan's a good kid. His brother was a good student and Ryan would always speak to me in the hallway last year."

"How old is he?"

"Probably sixteen or seventeen would be my guess. If he's taking our classes, he's somewhere in that range."

"Maybe I should introduce him to Rilan."

"Oh, he'd be a good one," Amy agreed. "Comes from a good family."

"That's one of the things I'm nervous about this year. I want Rilan to like it here."

"He will," Aaron chimed in. "And he has a lot of watchful eyes on him to make sure he settles into a good crowd."

"Thanks." Cade felt relieved and grateful for his new acquaintances. "I wasn't sure if this would be the right move for us, but I had to get him out of the city. Lots of reminders for him, because that's where he lived with his parents. And just us trying to adjust to the two of us. It was tough. Yes, we're still close by, but it's nice not to have to deal with some of the urban issues we were dealing with. Apartment living with a teenager is also hard." Cade smothered a smile with his hand. "Let's just say I was tired of paying noise violation tickets because Rilan likes heavy metal."

"Typical teenager," Amy reported. "I went through that phase."

"I think we all did," Aaron admitted. "Now I can hardly stand it."

"Likewise." Amy grinned as Cade eased onto the couch and helped himself to a slice of pizza. She could see the tension he tried to mask; his shoulders tight, he perched on the edge of the cushion as if ready to take flight at a moment's notice. "You plan on staying a while, Wickerson?" Amy teased and pointed to his awkward sitting position.

He looked up, the stringy cheese from his pizza dangling between his mouth and the slice. He took an oversized bite to prevent a mess and then barely chewed before swallowing. "What do you mean?"

"You look like you're ready to spring out of here any minute now." Amy smiled as she spoke, but she nestled into the other end of the couch, deep into the cushion with her legs folded under her.

"Oh. No, I'm fine."

"Give him a break, Ames. He just didn't want to sit near you and is being polite," Aaron jested and then grimaced when Amy punched him in the shoulder as he leaned toward the pizza box to grab his own slice of pizza.

"Just want him to feel comfortable," Amy replied.

"I do. I am. I'm just… I guess I'm just a little on edge about tomorrow. I probably won't sleep a wink," Cade admitted.

"First day jitters." Rachel shook her head in sympathy as she sat in one of the free chairs.

"You'll be fine." Amy waved his concerns away. "Besides, you will have me across the hall if you need anything."

Cade forced a smile, but his nerves lingered.

"You really are nervous." Amy leaned toward him and rested a hand on his arm. "You're going to do great. The kids are going to love you. Trust me, I was across the hall from your predecessor for six years. The kids are going to be excited about the change."

Cade held her encouraging gaze a moment longer before exhaling a deep breath that ended in a more relaxed smile. "I guess you're right. This will be my fifth school in seven years. I should be used to new places and faces. I think I'm more nervous than Rilan. To be honest, most of my nerves comes from hoping he excels here as well. He despised his last school, so I'm just feeling the pressure."

"He'll do great," Aaron said. "He's a good kid. Most of the kids here are good kids. Good families. He'll find some friends."

Amy patted his arm then retreated to her spot on the other end of the couch before hopping to her feet. "I'm going to grab another bottle. Anyone else?"

Aaron raised his hand.

Cade stood and followed her to the kitchen. She reached into the refrigerator and grabbed two bottles of beer. When she closed the door and turned, Cade stood in her path. She gasped and fumbled a moment in surprise, and he reached out to catch one of the bottles before it crashed against the floor. She held a hand to her racing heart.

"Sorry about that."

She reached for the bottle and he held onto it a bit longer. Her eyes flashed up to his, a touch of confusion hidden in their depths.

"I just wanted to say thank you, Amy." He released the bottle.

"For what?"

He sighed as he slipped his hands into his pant pockets and rocked back on his heels. "For your willingness to help me out if I need it."

"I don't think you will," she admitted.

He smirked. "You're confident, then."

She tilted her head and studied him a moment.

"Um, guys," Aaron called to the kitchen and had them both jolting to attention. "My drink?" Aaron asked.

"Got it." Amy held it up and nervously bypassed Cade to walk back towards the living room. Aaron winked at Cade as Amy squeezed by Rachel to find her seat again. She then handed the beer to Aaron and Cade kicked himself for making Aaron think there was something brewing between Amy and himself. And though he felt a slight tug in his chest when he thought about her, he wasn't quite ready to admit that's where his mind was headed also.

∞

Amy took a deep breath and sighed as she listened for the first bell to ring to start the first class of the day. She exited the teacher's lounge and made her way toward her classroom.

The final bell rang for first period to start. She spotted Cade at his door greeting his students as they walked in, all the teenage girls batting their eye lashes at him. Amy grinned, then scratched the beard she wore on her face.

Cade glanced at her with a confused expression, followed by a familiar grin. He burst into laughter as she walked up to him. "You ready for your first class at P.S. 14, Wickerson?"

"Is that you Ms. Frasier? I could hardly tell under all that scruff." He lightly rubbed his fingers over her fake beard.

She swatted his hand away. "I'm not Ms. Frasier right now, Mr. Wickerson. I'm Abraham Lincoln."

He burst into laughter again, causing the students in both their classes to lean forward in their desks to look at them through the doorways.

"Of course. My apologies, sir. My, how you have shrunk over the centuries!"

She couldn't help the laugh that bubbled forth. She playfully swatted his arm but then squeezed his hand, her eyes kind. "Your classroom looks great." She complimented his decorations. "Good luck today."

She let go slowly and walked into her room with a loud and boisterous man voice that made him smile even bigger. He walked into his room and clapped his hands ready for the day.

Amy entered her room. "Some of you may not know who I am," Amy stated in as deep a voice as she could muster. "The last time you studied me was in your 8th grade U.S. History class." The students all grinned as they watched her walk back and forth at the front of the classroom in her tailored tuxedo, beard, and top hat. "Abe Lincoln is my name. I was the sixteenth President of the United States. You last left me hangin' out in the history books during the Civil War. Now, who can tell me what they know about the Civil War?"

Several students raised their hands and Amy called on them. "You must stand, kind sir, state your name, your favorite band, and one fact you know of said war." She gestured dramatically.

The student stood with a large grin on his face. "I'm Toby Thompson, Raging Sea Monkeys are by far my favorite band, and my one fact of the Civil War is that it was between the North and the South."

"Also known as…" Amy prodded.

"The Union and the Confederacy."

"Very good, Mr. Thompson." Amy lightly pulled her beard down off her face to show herself underneath. "And I love the Raging Sea Monkeys too," she stated in her regular voice with excitement before replacing the beard and turning back into Abe Lincoln. Several students giggled. She loved that sound. History and humor. "Now, who else can tell me what they know of the Civil War?"

More hands shot up, this time in excitement, making Amy smile. Good ol' Abe Lincoln was a hit.

∞

Cade turned as he walked up to his podium; he spotted Amy continuing her lesson as Abe Lincoln and smiled. "Okay, so we are going to play a bit of a game to help me learn your names and to create our seating chart. I want everyone to stand up, grab your things, and move to this side of the room." He motioned toward the right side of the classroom.

"Okay, you." He pointed to a blonde-haired, blue eyed beauty queen who perked up at his acknowledgment. "What's your name?"

"Melissa."

"Melissa. Class, this is Melissa, it's nice to meet you Melissa, I am Mr. Wickerson. Please have a seat there." He motioned to the first desk, which she sat in gladly as he penciled her name on his chart.

He motioned to the next student. "Ryan."

"Ryan, nice to see you again, man." He shook the young pizza delivery boy's hand, "This is Melissa, and you know who I am. Please have a seat behind Melissa, Ryan." The tall lanky kid slid in behind the bombshell with a smile. Cade winked at him before continuing, knowing the kid was very pleased with his seat.

Cade carried on his introductions, reintroducing every student to the previous students and himself until the very end.

"And you?"

"Carter."

"Carter, it is nice to meet you." Cade took a deep breath and wriggled his eyebrows as he stood at the front of the room. "Okay, who thinks I can remember all of your names?" He stepped away from the podium to avoid cheating and glancing at his now filled in chart.

Several hands went up while others remained doubtful.

"Carter, I would like you to meet Melissa, Ryan, Sarah, Anthony, Chase, Bobby, Terrance, Shanna, Taylor, Anna, Peyton, Reese, Oscar, Stephanie, Brittany," Cade took another deep breath as he continued to point at students, "Rylie, Chris, Reagan, and Tucker. I am Mr. Wickerson, and it is nice to meet you."

The students cheered and clapped as Cade took a bow. "Thank you, thank you. We shall see if I remember them correctly tomorrow. Now welcome to English Literature. This is a class you cannot be shy in. We will be reading plays, sonnets, poems, books. You name it, we are going to cover it." He noticed several students roll their eyes, mainly the boys. "Now don't roll your eyes." He laughed and crossed his arms as he sat on the stool behind his podium. "Some of the best people love talking about literature. It's a great conversation starter. It teaches us about culture and history, while often entertaining us."

"Pretty sure I don't sit and discuss poems with my friends, and I don't know anyone who does," Terrance interrupted. Cade exaggerated his displeasure and shook his head. "Hold that thought, then. Let me grab Ms. Frasier for a moment, a perfect specimen to help illustrate my point."

Cade darted across the hall and knocked on Amy's door. She glanced over at him with her top hat slightly tilted on her head. "Mr. Wickerson, may I help you?"

She walked over with worry in her eyes. "Is everything okay?" she whispered.

He nodded with a gleam in his eye as he straightened her hat. "Yes, Ms. Frasier. I wondered if I could borrow you for just one second?" She looked at him with concern still lingering in her gaze and turned to her students.

"Okay, I want each of you to take turns writing a fact about the Civil War or Abraham Lincoln on the board. Start with the first person in each row, and as they sit the next person may go. I'll be just one second."

She walked across the hall with Cade preparing herself to lecture the students on their behavior, but as soon as they entered his classroom, Cade gently grabbed her hand and eased her into his stool. His students giggled softly as they watched, some leaning eagerly in their seats. "Ms. Frasier," Cade began. "Wait..." He rolled his desk chair near Amy and leaned back, propping his feet up on one of the students' desks as if he were hanging out with friends. His students laughed until Cade began to speak:
"If Love it's not, O God, what feel I so?
If Love it is, what sort of thing is he?
If Love be good, from where then comes my woe?
If he be ill, wondrous it seems to me
That every torment and adversity
That comes from him I can so joyous think;

For more I thirst, the more from him I drink."

He quoted the passage, inflection perfectly placed, his voice calm and confident, his words fluid, and his eyes dancing. Amy sat speechless. She opened her mouth to speak but nothing came out, unsure of why he quoted a passage on love to her in front of his class. Cade turned toward his class and winked as they giggled and clapped. When they quieted, Amy regained her senses. "Are you quoting Chaucer to me, Wickerson?"

He nodded and snapped his fingers as he plopped his feet to the floor and stood, and gently draped his arm around her shoulders. "Ms. Frasier, how did you know that was Geoffrey Chaucer?"

Amy turned to him confused. "Because I love Chaucer, and we discussed his work the other day."

Cade snapped his fingers and pointed at Terrance. "And there you have it. Friends do sit around and chat about literature. Not always, but its more relevant than you think. You can learn a lot about a person based on what they like or dislike. Or from certain poems, as you say, Terrance. You see, literature is magical. It speaks to us in ways nothing else can. A favorite book, a favorite character. We relate to literature in a way that is deep and personal. Ms. Frasier loves Geoffrey Chaucer. I know this as a fact. I just took a quote from one of his most famous works Troilus and Criseyde. She recognized it immediately because that work speaks to her personally. Do you understand where I am going with this?"

The students nodded. A slow smile spread over Amy's face as she realized he was trying to share his love of literature with the students.

"Thank you, Ms. Frasier, for being such a good sport. You can go back to being Abe Lincoln now." He tapped the top of her hat, making the students laugh.

"Yes, well," She had her Abe Lincoln voice again. "Anytime, Mr. Wickerson. A president is always happy to serve his people."

The students and Cade laughed as she made her way back across the hall.

"So, Mr. Wick," another one of the students began, "Will we have to memorize passages?"

"Yes, some you will. You will also write passages, sonnets, and poems." And thankfully, to his credit, not one student grumbled about the task.

CHAPTER SEVEN

Throughout the day, Amy caught Cade glancing across the hall and watching her teach. Her face blushed each time, thinking of his quote from earlier and the perfect recitation in which he performed it. Exchanging smiles throughout the day, along with air high fives, she could not remember the last time she had taught a full day with such excitement. When the final bell rang, her students began filing out and she stood in the hallway outside her door.

"See you tomorrow, Ms. Frasier!" several students called as they shouldered their backpacks and left. Cade stood in the hallway as well, several of his male students from earlier in the day walking by and giving him a high five or a fist bump. "Later, Mr. Wick."

As the hallway emptied, Amy smirked. "Sounds like you had a good day today."

"I did. It was a blast. How about you...er, I mean, Abe?"

She laughed as she slipped the hat off her head. She pulled the beard off her face, her cheeks reddened by the scratchiness of the hair. "It was good. Exhausting talking in a man voice all day, but I'll get used to it."

"Do you talk in a man voice often?"

She laughed not realizing how her comment had sounded. "Actually yeah, I guess I do. Most historical figures we cover are men, so I try to act accordingly."

"Do you dress up every day?"

"No, not every day, but quite often. I find it holds their attention and initiates a level of eagerness and excitement in the topic. And for the visual learners, it helps them retain the visual along with the information."

"I like your style, Frasier."

"And I like yours, Wickerson. Although, I was a bit worried at first when you began reciting love quotes to me. I mean, we hardly know each other." She playfully held her hand on her heart and mocked a swoon.

He laughed. "Yes, well, I was making a point, and thankfully you reacted naturally and convincingly enough to prove it. I thank you." His eyes sparkled as his smile warmed her.

"Yes, well... anytime," she mumbled and headed into her classroom.

Cade watched her closely as she grabbed her purse and locked up her door. She waited as he did the same. Rilan walked up with his backpack draped over one shoulder.

"Hey kid. How was your first day?"

He shrugged his shoulders. "Pretty good, I guess. I liked your class."

"Why, thank you," she replied in Abe's voice.

Rilan grinned at her antics and allowed her to drape her arm over his shoulder.

Cade put his arm over Rilan's shoulders as well, his arm landing on top of Amy's in the process. "I'm glad you had a good day."

"Did you?" Rilan looked up at his uncle.

"I did. I think it was a success."

Amy smiled at Cade and squeezed Rilan's shoulders. "So, did you meet any cool friends?"

"Yeah, I met a couple of guys. Ryan and Toby."

"Ah, yay, they are good kids," she replied, more for Cade's ears than Rilan's.

"Yeah, they were pretty cool."

"Did you meet any pretty girls?"

Rilan rolled his eyes and Amy laughed.

Suzanne Meters rounded the corner of the hallway and her eyes widened at the camaraderie between Amy, Cade, and Rilan.

"Oh, hello there, Mr. Wickerson. How was your first day?"

They all stopped their trek and waited, Cade not removing his arm from Amy's.

"It was great. I think I am going to like it here."

She smiled widely at his announcement and then her gaze turned to Amy and hardened. "I see you were Abe Lincoln today, Ms. Frasier. Nice outfit."

Amy forced a polite smile and nodded. "Thanks."

"Why is your face red?" Suzanne asked, calling out what she hoped to be a flaw.

"My beard." Amy rubbed her hand over her jaw line at the raw skin.

Cade laughed, remembering the patchy fake hair she had stuck to her face all day.

"Oh sweetie, they make creams for that," Suzanne added venomously.

Cade's smile faded as he realized Suzanne's intention to make Amy feel embarrassed.

Amy shrugged. "I'm an all-natural kind of gal." She winked at Cade and then nodded toward the exit.

He grinned on a nod. "Well, we are heading home Suzanne. See you tomorrow."

She stepped aside and watched as they all three left in each other's arms.

"I don't like her," Rilan announced as soon as they stepped outside.

Amy burst into laughter and squeezed his shoulders in a light hug. "Oh, Rilan. I love your honesty."

"Yes, well, best keep that opinion to yourself," Cade warned him. "And still respect her in the hallways."

"I will. Just wanted it on record."

Amy laughed again, causing Cade to do the same. "She is an acquired taste."

As they reached the parking lot, Amy glanced around and her smile faded. She had ridden to school with Aaron, and she now noticed his truck was gone. He had left her behind knowing she would need to catch a ride with Cade. She shook her head in annoyance. "Um, guys…"

"Yeah?" they both asked, turning toward her.

"You think I could hitch a ride with you guys? Aaron seems to have left me."

"Of course." Cade unlocked his truck and opened the front passenger door for her, Rilan sliding in the back seat. Pleased that she would be willing to ride with him again after their small accident the last time, he rounded the front of the truck, slid behind the wheel and pointed them toward home.

∞

Pulling into Amy's driveway, another truck sat on the curb. "Who is that?" Rilan's question floated through the air as Amy muffled a soft groan.

"It's Coach Stanton." She forced a cheerfulness into her tone as she slipped out of the truck. Eric walked across the lawn, surprise on his face at seeing Amy riding with Cade.

"Amy." He offered a polite wave to Cade.

"What brings you by, Eric?"

"I was hoping to take you to dinner tonight since you couldn't make it out the other night due to your migraine. We could celebrate a successful first day of school."

Cade saw the dread creep over Amy's face, but he wasn't sure if an intervention would be appropriate on his part, so he waited. Her door remained ajar, and her bag sat in his floorboard, so his hopes of making the situation less awkward were dashed. "I'm actually pretty worn out after today."

"Then not having to cook dinner will be a good thing." Eric clapped his hands and placed a hand at the small of her back, already leading her toward his truck.

"Wait." Amy stopped. "I have to at least grab my stuff from Cade's truck. Give me a second."

She walked over and leaned inside Cade's vehicle with a tired smile. "Thanks for the ride, you two. I'm glad you both had a great first day of school. I'll see you tomorrow." She grabbed her bag and shot Cade a regretful glance.

He reached over and grabbed her hand as she gripped her bag. Looking up, Amy eyed him curiously. "You could always tell him no," he stated softly.

Amy's cheeks flushed at having Rilan witness their conversation and she slowly eased her hand away. "It's okay. I owe it to him." Shrugging her shoulders, she draped her bag on her arm. "Thanks again." She shut the door and walked toward Eric, the man exuberant as he opened the passenger door to his truck.

"So, I take it Amy isn't a fan of the coach?" Rilan asked.

"Ms. Frasier," Cade corrected.

"Listen, Uncle Cade, her name is Amy. I'll call her Ms. Frasier at school, but it's just weird calling her that outside of school. Besides, she told me to call her Amy the first time I met her."

Cade didn't respond.

"I think if you were to have made up something, you could have saved her from an evening with that guy."

"It's not my place."

"Why not? You're friends, aren't you?"

"I would like to think so, but we're still new here, Rilan. I don't know the dynamics of their friendship or what Amy would actually prefer."

"I think she'd prefer dinner with you over that guy."

"Why's that?" Cade asked.

"Because you totally dig her."

Gawking at his nephew, Cade turned in his seat. "And what makes you say that?"

"Because it's obvious."

"I sure hope not. We work together. That would be inappropriate."

"It isn't stopping that guy. They work together."

"It's different."

"Not really."

Frustrated, Cade huffed and turned his truck on. "Yes, well, it's not going to happen. And no, I'm not interested in Ms. Frasier. We're just friends."

Rilan relaxed against his seat and adjusted his seat belt. "Whatever you say, Uncle Cade. But I feel bad for her. She didn't want to go to dinner with him."

"Then she could have said no."

"She's too nice," Rilan explained.

"And you seem to be an expert on Ms. Frasier and what she wants or needs. I'm sure she would appreciate your concern. But guard your words, Rilan. It's none of our business."

Rilan held up his hands in surrender. "Fine. Just trying to help."

"There's no need for it," Cade added as he cast one last look at Amy and Eric pulling away from the curb. Amy lifted her hand in a small wave as she passed them, and he kicked himself for not doing what Rilan suggested.

CHAPTER EIGHT

Amy walked into the restaurant wearing the stupid tuxedo she wore at school that day. She hadn't even been able to go home to change, and though she could tell Eric was disappointed by some of the stares they received, he didn't say a word. She looked tired and crumpled. Not the kind of Amy he had probably hoped to see tonight, but it was her. She'd spent the majority of her day portraying Abe Lincoln and she loved it. She loved dressing up as some of the people throughout history. If Eric had given her just a few minutes at home, she could have changed, but all was well. She was starving and this did relieve the annoyance of whipping up dinner at home.

He smiled as he sat across from her at a small table in the center of the room. "Thanks for agreeing to come with me to Romero's. How was your first day of school?"

"No problem. It's one of my favorite places. And today was tiring, but great. You?"

He shrugged. "Pretty good. I wasn't super impressed with my lineup of athletes, but who knows, maybe they will grow... a lot."

She chuckled as the waitress came forward and asked for their order. Amy ordered a plate of spaghetti and a side Caesar salad and then politely handed the woman her menu.

"Becca? Becca is that you?" An older man reached out and grasped Amy's forearm on the table, causing Eric to stiffen.

Amy turned to the loving and desperate gaze of an old man sitting in a wheelchair, an old blanket draped over his lap. "No, I'm sorry. I'm Amy. What's your name?"

The old man smiled. "It's me, honey. I've been looking everywhere for you, Becca."

Amy's brow furrowed as a young gentleman rushed over. "Grandpa, there you are. I apologize,

Miss. My Grandpa suffers from a severe case of Alzheimer's. Grandpa, our table is over here."

The handsome grandson tried to steer the man away from their table, but his grasp on Amy's arm tightened.

"Grandpa, she is not Becca. Let go of her arm." The young man tapped his Grandpa's hand and cast another apologetic glance her way.

"You come from the circus again?" The old man asked Amy, his eyes roaming over her wardrobe.

Amy couldn't help the laugh that bubbled up. "No, actually I didn't, but I definitely look like a circus act, don't I?"

The old man chuckled, his frail frame shaking as he did. His grip softened, and he looked at Amy with true love in his eyes, making her gasp. "Becca, my love, may we have one last dinner together before I leave town?"

The hope in the man's eyes had her glancing toward Eric, who wore a scowl. Her heart melted at this old man and whoever this Becca was that touched his heart. "I would love to." She squeezed his hand in return and glanced at the grandson.

"You don't have to do this," the young man stated.

"Yes, I do," Amy replied softly and extended her hand. "Amy Frasier."

The man shook her hand and smiled. "Peter Hollings. Nice to meet you."

"Nice to meet you as well. This is Eric Stanton." She motioned to Eric. Eric stood, which Amy thought very polite, until he glanced at her with heat in his gaze and walked away without a glance back.

She and Peter stood with mouths open in shock. "I am so sorry," they stated at the same time.

Amy lightly patted the hand he rested on his grandfather's wheelchair. "Don't be. I didn't want to eat with him anyway. Honestly, you rescued me. Please, join me."

The old man's smile lit up when he glanced at Amy. "Becca you grow more beautiful by the day."

"Why thank you—" She looked to Peter.

"James."

"James," she finished. "I love your tie. Is it new?"

The old man glanced down and nodded toward Peter. "Yes, I got it last Christmas from Peter."

Amy looked to Peter and smiled.

"Grandpa, I bought you that tie in 94'," he corrected.

The old man's smile faltered slightly. "Well, it seems like only yesterday."

Amy's heart ached for the older man and warmed at the younger man sitting across from her.

The waitress walked up and held a look of confusion as she held plates for Amy and Eric. "I will cover the cost of both dishes, but my previous companion has left. I'm sorry gentlemen, but I already ordered my—"

"Oh Becca. Chicken parmesan, my favorite!" James exclaimed and reached for Eric's plate. Amy nodded, and the woman placed the food in front of them.

"And for you, sir?"

"I will just share with my grandpa, thank you," Peter stated.

"Amy, I apologize again for interfering with your evening. My grandpa seems to find you quite intriguing."

She laughed. "I think the feeling is mutual."

She smiled sweetly at the older man as he completely forgot about his food and began snoozing in his chair. Peter slid the plate to himself and began cutting the chicken.

"You come here often?" Amy asked.

Peter shook his head. "No, I am just here visiting my grandfather. We used to come here when I was a kid, and it's one of the few places he remembers."

"I see. That's kind of you to come see him. I'm sure he is grateful."

Peter relaxed in his chair as he watched her take a sip of her drink. "What about you?"

"I would like to say no, but I probably eat here once every week or so. It's sort of a local spot for my friends and me."

"Like the gentleman who just left?"

"Oh, he is not my friend. Well, more of an acquaintance. We work together."

Peter nodded in understanding. A moment of silence passed between them.

"So, where are you from?" Amy asked, twirling noodles around her fork.

"San Francisco."

Her eyes widened. "Wow, yes, I guess that is a trip for you, then."

"It is, but it's quite worth it." He smiled tenderly at the snoring man beside them.

Amy lightly rubbed the old man's arm as he slept. "He's a sweet man."

Peter watched her intently, liking everything about the charming woman who did not seem the least bit annoyed by their abrupt interruption.

"What's your story, Amy?" he asked kindly.

She turned to face him again and shrugged. "I'm a teacher, which explains my incredibly embarrassing wardrobe at the moment. I was Abe Lincoln today."

His eyes widened in amusement. "And where is your hat?"

"In the car. Literally, I have a hat and a beard. Which I'm assuming will show up mysteriously in my classroom tomorrow morning since I rode with Eric."

"A beard?" Peter laughed heartily. "Now that is indeed charming. And I hope he returns it to you."

"Yes, well, if I knew I would be meeting two handsome strangers tonight I would have attempted to go home and change," she said, laughing at herself and her blunder.

Peter took her compliment in stride. "Well, I think it looks quite dashing. A little eccentric, but then again, I'm from San Francisco. I'm used to eccentric."

A large smile bloomed across her face. "I like you, Peter. You are a breath of fresh air after sitting here awkwardly with Eric for ten minutes." She covered her mouth as soon as the comment flew out. "I am so sorry. That was rude of me. Please forget I said that."

Laughing, Peter pulled her hand away from her mouth. "Trust me, I do not find it rude at all. I take it as a compliment."

She blushed under his scrutiny, pulled her hand away, and ate a bite of her spaghetti.

They chatted for another hour before the waitress finally cleared their plates and left the black tab folder on their table. Peter reached for it and placed his credit card in the slot and handed it back to the woman.

"Oh no, please allow me to pay for it." Amy reached for her wallet in her purse.

Peter held up his hand. "No, Amy, please allow me to buy your dinner. You not only took my grandfather's assault with kindness but have listened to him snore for the last hour, and you have politely engaged in conversation with me while he sleeps. Believe me, it is my pleasure."

She stared into his dark brown eyes, noting the kindness that shimmered there and finally nodded. "Alright, well thank you."

He lightly nudged his grandpa's arm, the old man jerking awake and yelling for someone named Lucille. When he glanced up at his grandson, his gaze grew foggy. "Bill, is that you?"

"No, Grandpa, I'm Peter. Bill's son, remember?"

"Oh right, Peter. My, you have grown up into a handsome young man. How old are you these days? Thirty?"

Peter calmly wrapped the worn plaid blanket tighter around his grandfather's legs as a sadness fluttered through his gaze. "Thirty-four, Grandpa."

"My goodness, is this your bride?" He motioned to Amy with a large smile. Peter blushed at the comment. "No, Grandpa, she is just a friend. Her name is Amy."

"You have beautiful friends."

Peter chuckled with Amy as he began pushing his grandfather's wheelchair.

As they stepped outside, Amy watched as Peter began making his way to a silver SUV. He turned and smiled. "Thank you again, Amy, for a great dinner. Again, I am sorry for the intrusion. But I have to say, I rather enjoyed getting to know you." His warm gaze travelled over her odd outfit, and she flourished her hand in front of her as she bowed. He chuckled.

"Likewise. Perhaps next time you are in town we can do it again."

He smiled. "Yes, I would like that."

"Becca!" James turned around and grabbed Amy's arm again and kissed her hand. He pulled her toward him and gently cupped her face in his soft, wrinkly hands. "Oh, my Becca, you are gorgeous. You always have been. I'm sorry my love, but Bill has to take me to the home now. Will I see you next week?"

Amy looked up to Peter, mixed emotions in his gaze.

"Maybe so, James. Maybe so," she answered lightly.

The old man pulled her towards him and kissed her firmly and passionately on the lips. When he let go, Amy stumbled back a bit. Peter flushed. "I am so sorry," he whispered in horror as he scooped up his grandfather and eased him into the passenger seat.

Amy chuckled and lightly covered her lips with her fingertips. "My, I haven't been kissed like that in a while!"

Peter chuckled nervously, running a hand through his dark brown hair. "I really don't know what to say after that just happened."

They both laughed as Amy gave him a light hug. "We will just end it on a good note, how about that?"

Peter agreed and gave a slight nod toward her, years of prep school showing in his demeanor. "You are a sweet woman, Amy. I thank you."

She waved. "Oh, Peter?"

"Yes?" he asked, sliding into the driver seat.

"Who is Becca?"

A slow, sad smile fluttered over his face. "My grandmother. She passed away ten years ago."

A sudden sadness filled Amy's heart for James as she shifted her gaze to look at him through the back window, sound asleep. Peter shut his door, his window down. Amy leaned in and lightly kissed him on the cheek. "Thank you, Peter, for a very sweet evening with James."

Peter nodded, both of them choked up by the happenings of the evening. He slowly backed out and gave one last wave to Amy as she walked back inside the restaurant to make a phone call to Rachel to come pick her up.

∞

Rachel pulled into Aaron's driveway and hopped out. "We were having our own first day of school party without you," Rachel admitted.

Cade's brows rose as Amy stepped out onto the back porch with Rachel and she waved in greeting, her smile slightly tainted by a touch of sadness.

"And how was your night out with Eric?" Aaron asked, handing her a beer.

Amy shook her head.

"That bad, huh?" he asked.

"Actually, my evening went extremely well, but not with Eric."

"What?" Aaron asked.

Amy sighed a deep contented breath. "Yeah. I met the most amazing men tonight."

Cade's eyebrows arched at her statement and a sly grin travelled over Aaron's face. "Men? As in plural?"

Amy chuckled. "Yes, men. I was sitting with Eric at this table and an old man was being wheeled past me in a wheelchair by his grandson, Peter. The old man grabbed my arm and began calling me by his wife's name. The man suffers from Alzheimer's, and he truly thought I was his wife from long ago. His grandson, Peter, is so sweet and friendly. They just melted my heart. Needless to say, when James, the grandfather, asked me if he could eat with me, I said yes. Of course, Eric didn't like that, so he stood up and left."

"He walked out?" Cade asked in shock, choking on his beer.

She nodded sadly. "Yes, he did. I felt terrible for Peter and James. Peter kept apologizing, but I waved it off. He had no need. I ended up having the most refreshing dinner date in a long time." She lightly held her hand to her heart. "He was the sweetest man."

"The grandson or the grandfather?" Aaron asked with a chuckle.

"Grandfather, although Peter was very sweet too."

"What did Peter look like?" Rachel asked with a wink.

"Oh, he was handsome," Amy explained. "But not really my type."

"Why?"

Amy just ignored her question and took a sip of her beer, a smile spreading over her face.

"What are you thinking about?" Aaron prodded her for more information.

Amy chuckled at the memory. "After dinner I walked with them over to Peter's car and knelt before James to say goodbye. He grabbed my face and kissed me. Quite passionately, might I add."

Cade grinned at the thought of an old man kissing Amy. His heart warmed at her tenderness toward the man.

"You're a sweetheart," he complimented softly as he took another sip of his beer. She thanked him with her tender gaze.

"I'm glad you had a good evening, but you will have to make it up to Eric," Rachel stated.

Amy looked at her friend with distaste. "Yes, well, we will see about that. He left, my school bag still in his car and everything. Not a word. He was not exactly friendly to James or Peter."

"Well, would you be if another woman interrupted your date and insisted on eating with you?"

"They did not insist on eating with us!" Amy lost her temper as she glared at Rachel. "James asked me, and if you had seen the love in that old man's eyes you would have done the exact same thing! Eric was rude. He didn't even introduce himself or listen to James' story. He just left. And if that is the type of guy he is, then I will *not* apologize to him or make it up to him!"

Amy stood and grabbed her purse. "I think I will just call it a night. I'm exhausted, and I had an amazing evening and would like to enjoy it. I will see you guys tomorrow." She walked back into the house and grabbed her purse, planning to just walk the last couple of blocks home.

Cade finished his beer and stood quickly. "I'm going to try and catch her for a second." He darted after her.

"What was that about?" Aaron asked Rachel.

She shrugged. "I think Amy needs to apologize to Eric, that's all."

"Why? He was obviously rude to those men."

"Because she needs to see where things go with him. He's liked her for years. I think she owes him a decent night out and a chance."

"Why? We both know he is not her type of guy."

"No, Aaron, we do not both know. She's never dated anyone in the years I've known her. When was the last time she dated someone seriously?"

Aaron shrugged. "It doesn't matter. She is happy by herself. Why is that so hard to understand?"

"She is not happy by herself," Rachel argued. "She's content having you."

"What?!" Aaron's face reddened. "What are you talking about? Amy and I are just friends."

"Yes, you are, but she doesn't need a boyfriend when she has a guy best friend."

Aaron stood from his chair. "I think you are looking at this from the wrong perspective. Amy is a great friend to both of us. She loves us. Just because she chooses not to date anyone does not mean she uses me as a crutch."

Rachel rubbed a hand over her face. "You're right. I just... Eric *is* a nice guy. And he's been interested in Amy a long time. I just hate for people not to receive a fair chance."

"Sounds like Eric had one. He had an opportunity to show kindness to others and he didn't take it. That right there will speak volumes for Ames. We have to trust her judgment and that she knows what's best for herself."

He tapped his bottle to hers and stood. "Besides, I have a feeling Cade isn't going to let Amy slip through his fingers for very long."

"I sense some chemistry there as well. But again, I'm not sure if Amy will pursue it," Rachel added.

Shrugging, Aaron walked toward the door. "I'm going to grab another beer. Want one?"

She nodded and took the last couple of sips of the one she held as she watched him walk inside.

∞

Cade caught Amy's elbow as she stepped out the front door of Aaron's house and onto the porch. She turned in surprise. "Hey."

"Let me walk you home," he offered.

"That's okay. It's not far."

"It's late. I'd feel better if you let me walk you home or drive you."

Her lips quirked, and she nodded. "Alright. Let's walk."

She led the way down the front steps and waited at the edge of the sidewalk for him.

"So, tell me more about James."

She sighed, pleased that he would ask. "He was so sweet, Cade. He had the most loving gaze. I'm pretty sure I have never been looked at like that before, and I probably never will be again. He had so much love in his eyes for me, thinking I was his wife, Becca. My heart just melted. His grandson, Peter, was so kind as well. Caring. I couldn't turn that man away, not in a million years. No matter who was sitting at the table with me, I would have accepted his dinner invitation. And he kissed me with so much love. I know it sounds weird that an old man's kiss could make my heart burst into happiness, but it was different than a kiss of attraction. This was pure love. I can't explain it. It made my heart ache for him at his loss, but so happy for him too, because who has that kind of love these days? Not many."

She glanced over at him, and his soft smile encouraged her to continue.

"It was so touching, Cade. I cannot think of any other way to describe it."

Cade's arm brushed hers and she slipped her arm through his in companionable silence. She hadn't realized tears were clouding her eyes until she felt them slide down her cheeks. She reached up and dabbed them quickly away. She wasn't expecting such an incredible encounter with a stranger tonight, but James's love for Becca touched her deeply. She wanted to know their history. And their love story. Such history deserved to be known and shared, even if it was just to a group of students or her friends.

Cade paused and turned toward her. He reached up and gently brushed the tears from her cheeks and pulled her into a hug. "You look like you need one of these."

She bit back a soft sob as she embraced him in return and buried her cheek against his chest.

"You were blessed by James and Peter tonight. I'm glad you accepted their invitation and befriended James. How light his heart must have felt at the sight of his beloved."

His calm words soothed her soul; her eyes looked up at him and his warm gaze eased her concerns over facing Eric at school the next day.

Amy stood on her tip toes and lightly touched her lips to his cheek. Shyly, she eased back to her heels. It was a sweet, short, and gentle caress that left her breathless and vulnerable. "Thank you, Cade."

"You're welcome." They continued walking. "I wish I had the pleasure of meeting them tonight."

They reached her house, and he walked her up the two steps leading to her front door. "I will let you get some rest." He squeezed her hand before walking back the direction in which he came, his hands in his pockets.

"Cade," Amy called after him, stepping onto the porch as he stood in the yard.

He turned around.

"Want to carpool tomorrow?"

A large smile bloomed on his face. "I'd like that."

She nodded with an excited smile on her face and waved as he turned toward the direction of his house. She sighed as she closed the door, and bit back a content smile that had her floating down the hallway to her bedroom. She rubbed a hand over her face and felt the scruffiness of the glue and remnants of her daily beard. "It was a good night, Abe. A good night." She grinned as she took a washcloth and began to gently scrub her face.

CHAPTER NINE

Suzanna walked by Cade's classroom and leaned in to see if he was inside. Seeing the empty space, she turned to leave and spotted him walking into the teachers' lounge and straight to the drink machine. Slipping his change into the coin slot, he punched the soda button and waited.

Aaron walked up and lightly patted him on the back. "How's it going, man?"

Cade grinned and followed him to a round table and sat. "Going pretty good." His smile grew as Rachel walked up and greeted them, sliding into a chair and peeling an orange.

"Where's Amy?" she asked as she glanced around.

"Probably in her room," Aaron began. "She was hoping to prep a pop quiz for tomorrow."

"Ah. Third day of school. She's brave," Rachel chuckled.

"My, isn't this the fun table!" Suzanne Meter's voice carried over to them and she gazed at Amy's empty seat. "May I?" Without an invitation, she slid into the chair. "So, Mr. Wickerson, I heard some interesting news today: that Rilan is not your son, but your nephew?"

"That is correct." He took a bite of his sandwich and slipped a chip into his mouth.

"I'm pretty sure everyone thought he was your son," she giggled softly. "You two look so much alike. Oh, where is Amy, by the way? She out today?"

"She's in her classroom prepping for tomorrow," Rachel answered with a slight edge to her voice.

"Ah, I see." Suzanne leaned toward Cade. "So, Mr. Wickerson, I was wondering if you were attending the football game this Friday? First one of the season, you know."

"I am not sure, actually. I will have to see."

"Well, if you do," Suzanne jotted her phone number on a napkin and handed it to him. "You can sit by me. Just call me when you're out in front of the stadium and I'll come find you."

Cade choked on his bite and lightly patted his chest as Aaron and Rachel sat unimpressed by Suzanne. She slid from the seat and smiled. "Well, I must be getting back to my classroom. Have a nice lunch."

"What the—?" Rachel whispered. "You're going to have to shut that down, Cade. She's only going to get worse."

"What do I do? I don't encourage any of it," Cade defended.

Aaron laughed and then grunted at the punches he received from both Cade and Rachel. "Sorry man, it's just... I've been on the receiving end of Suzanne. It's hard to escape her clutches. Doable, but hard."

"Well, then tell me how, because she is not on my radar."

"You date someone else." Aaron shrugged as if the answer was simple.

"But you're not dating anyone else, are you?" Cade asked.

"Not at the moment, but I did when she was pursuing me, which sort of shut down her hopes of me being an option."

Cade rubbed a hand through his hair and blew a frustrated breath. "This is ridiculous."

Aaron just continued grinning as Rachel bit back a smile. "Welcome to P.S. 14," Aaron laughed.

"Can't we just teach together?" Cade asked.

Aaron shook his head. "Where's the fun in that? Especially when you can date and have your relationship on public display. And then break up and then have *that* on display."

Groaning, Cade just shook his head. "I think I'm going to pass on all of that."

Aaron laughed and Rachel just shook her head in dismay. "Not all relationships end, Aaron."

"No, they don't. But Suzanne?"

Rachel shrugged and she leaned toward Cade. "She does tend to filter through dates rather quickly."

"Good to know." Cade took a sip of his soda. "Thanks for the warning."

∞

Amy slipped her glasses off and rubbed her nose. "Six more, Frasier. Get it together," she whispered to herself, slipping her glasses back on her face. She heard a light knock on her door frame and glanced up.

"Hey, kid," she greeted Rilan as he walked in slowly with his lunch sack. "How's it going?"

"Mind if I eat with you?"

"Not at all. Come on in. Why aren't you eating with Ryan and Toby?"

"They had a UIL meeting, and well, they are sort of my only friends right now and I didn't want to sit at a table by myself in the cafeteria."

Understanding flashed over Amy's face and she smiled sweetly. "Well, I am grateful for the company. My brain was about to burst over these worksheets."

Smirking, he slid into the desk across from hers and opened his lunch. "So how was your date with Coach Stanton last night?"

Amy's eyes widened in surprise and her cheeks flushed at his question.

He laughed softly at her reaction and then smiled. "You don't have to tell me."

Amy smiled and shrugged. "There really wasn't one. He left before the food even made it to the table."

His eyes widened. "That bad at it, are you?"

"Hey now." Amy held a warning finger that made them both start to laugh. "There were extenuating circumstances."

"Did they involve my uncle?"

"No, why? What would make you think that?"

"You two just seemed quiet during the ride to school this morning. There was... tension."

"I'm sorry." She looked genuinely apologetic, and he shrugged. She then told him about James.

"You kissed an old guy?!" Shocked, he grimaced. "That's kind of gross."

Amy just shook her head and grinned. "It wasn't like that. And no, it was not gross. It was sweet."

"That's crazy, though, that his memories are all messed up. Kind of sad." Rilan took a bite of his sandwich and Amy nodded.

"Yeah, it kind of was."

"I can't imagine losing my memories. I mean, my memories of my mom and dad are scarce as it is. I can't imagine losing them completely." His voice sobered as he took a long swig of his soda and tried to hide the emotion in his tone.

"I'm sorry you lost your parents."

He shrugged. "It sucks. They were good people. My dad was awesome. He had the best laugh." Remembrance had him smirking. "Uncle Cade's a lot like him. Maybe that's why they left me to him."

"Could be," Amy admitted.

"I feel kind of bad for him, though, having to deal with me when he could be out partying and having a good time."

"And that's what you think he'd prefer to be doing?" Amy asked curiously.

Rilan shrugged. "Probably not. He'd probably be reading some boring old book and listening to soft jazz on the surround sound."

Amy chuckled and nodded in agreement. "I could see that."

"But I think he would definitely do more and be more social if he didn't have to worry about me at home."

"I think your uncle is quite content with how his life is going. And he loves you. You two have a unique bond, and I don't think he would trade that for the world."

"I know he wouldn't. Just something I think about, ya know?"

"Yeah." She smiled softly and waved her hand toward him to share his bag of chips. He tossed it to her, and she grabbed a few before handing them back. She set her glasses on the stack of papers on her desk.

"He seems to be fitting in here. As do you," Amy commented.

"I hope so. I'm determined to stick it out for his sake. We've moved a lot the last several years. It will be nice to stay in one place for a while."

Amy saw the boy's eyes glisten as he looked down at his sandwich and took a small bite.

"Well, I'm glad you came with him. I think I have a soft spot for you."

He chuckled around a sob, and she smiled. "I like you too," he admitted.

"Anytime you want to eat lunch in here, you're always welcome. So are your friends. I know the cafeteria can get loud and lame after a while."

He rolled his eyes. "Yesterday was awful. I didn't know where to go or where to sit. Thankfully, Ryan saw me floundering and saved me. But everyone stared at me like I was a zombie."

"You and zombies." Amy shook her head in mock dismay and made him snicker. "They'll get used to you. Before you know it, you won't have time to eat in here with me. I'll be all sad from the rejection."

She pretended to cry, and he rolled his eyes. "Maybe by then Uncle Cade will have finally asked you out and you can eat with him."

"Wait, what?" Amy sobered and Rilan wriggled his eyebrows. "Don't get any ideas, kid."

"Come on, Am— Ms. Frasier," he corrected. "You can't tell me you haven't thought about it."

"Excuse me?" she asked. "And what makes you think I've thought about it?"

"Haven't you?" he asked, studying her face to gauge her reaction. Not seeing the response he'd hoped for, his shoulders sagged. "It was just a thought."

A soft smile tilted her lips. "I'm glad you think it would be a good thing. I'm flattered. But your uncle probably just wants to get settled. And I'm his friend. Sometimes that's the best relationship to have with someone."

Rilan tilted his head in consideration. "Fine. I'll drop it for now."

She laughed. "Well, thank you."

∞

Cade walked back to his classroom and glanced into Amy's room. She laughed, and he realized someone sat across from her. Rilan. His heart swelled at the thought of them bonding.

"No way!" Amy responded to something Rilan had said and she laughed. "There is no way I would do that. I'd be scared."

Cade walked across the hall and leaned against her door frame and listened to their conversation.

"You have to. You know how impressed Uncle Cade would be if you did?"

"Impressed, huh?" Amy asked. "Are we back to that again?" She held a warning tone and his nephew grinned wickedly. "I'll think about it. I'm terrified of heights, kid, so he better be impressed if I decide to do it. Everyone better be."

Rilan chuckled and finished off his sandwich.

"Hey, you two," Cade greeted from the door.

Both straightened in their seats at his voice.

"What's going on in here? Party without me?"

He ruffled Rilan's hair before grabbing a seat on the corner of Amy's desk.

"Rilan was just sharing his cafeteria woes with me."

His eyebrows rose. "Is that so?" He looked at his nephew curiously.

"Yeah. No surprise, it's lame," Rilan reported dryly.

Cade laughed. "It'll get better."

Rilan stood and tossed his paper lunch sack in Amy's trash can. "Bell's about to ring. I've got to grab my book and head to Aaron's class."

Cade narrowed his eyes.

"Mr. Jacobs," Rilan corrected on a sigh.

Amy chuckled. "See you in sixth period, kid."

"Later." He punched Cade in the arm on his way out and headed down the hall.

"He okay?" Cade asked with worry.

She nodded. "Yes. You have a pretty amazing kid there, Cade."

"Yeah, he is," Cade stated proudly.

"And he loves you dearly."

Cade looked at her and smiled. "It's mutual. He hasn't had the easiest life."

"I don't think he sees it that way."

Cade's eyebrows rose again in surprise that Rilan had shared his past with her. "Well, thank you for letting him eat with you."

"He was good company, and I needed a break from papers. How was your lunch?"

"It was alright. Suzanne wants me to go to the football game with her Friday."

Amy laughed loudly. "And what did you say?"

"I said I would have to see."

"You would have to *see*?" Amy prodded with a smirk. "Interesting." She stroked her chin as if in thought.

His eyes narrowed and his lips twitched. "I was going to see if you normally go to the games before I said I would be there."

Amy laughed. "Me?"

He shrugged. "Yeah, do you go?"

"I planned to catch the game Friday," she said, nodding. "But I do not sit with Suzanne, usually."

"Don't think you could for one evening?" he asked.

She laughed. "Are you begging, Wickerson?"

"I guess I am."

"You could just go and sit wherever you want," Amy pointed out.

"I don't want to be rude," he admitted with a sigh. "Not going to lie, I feel a bit trapped."

"Don't blame you." She leaned forward in her chair and squeezed his hand. "Just go to the game, Cade. Sit wherever you want, with whomever you want. If Suzanne joins you, that's up to you, but it's your decision. You're being too nice about it all. If you don't want to sit with her, then tell her you have plans elsewhere. You can still be nice about it, but make your feelings clear."

He rubbed the back of his neck with his free hand. "I guess you're right." He brushed his thumb over her knuckles. "Thanks. Seems you're into helping Wickersons today."

Amy grinned. "All in a day's work." The bell rang and Cade slipped off her desk. "See you after school. I'm still taking you home?"

"You were my ride this morning," she pointed out.

"True."

Kids began filtering into the classroom and greeting them. Amy stood and rested a hand on his arm. "Go wow your students with words, Mr. Wickerson." She winked as he made his way to his classroom on a laugh.

CHAPTER TEN

The stadium bleachers shifted under the weighty and rowdy crowd. Yells, screams, whistles, and the stomping of feet to the cheerleaders' yells. All of it reminded Cade of his own time back in high school, and excitement drummed in his blood. He loved Friday night ball games growing up. The anticipation. The chance to hang out with friends and stay out later than his parents usually allowed. He spotted Aaron and Rachel and waved in greeting. He climbed the few rows to where they sat and shook hands with Aaron. "Glad you made it."

"Where's Rilan?" Rachel asked.

Cade pointed to his nephew, who tossed a nod toward one of the cheerleaders as she called his name in greeting.

"He's too cool to sit with me," Cade reported.

"Don't blame him." Amy's voice carried toward him as she walked up the bleachers and stood next to him. "Good to see you, Mr. Wickerson," she said with a grin.

"Ms. Frasier." He nodded as Suzanne made her way toward the bleachers and spotted them. Her eyes hardened a moment before she reached the bottom row. She then climbed her way up to them and smiled. "I'm so glad you made it." She rested a hand on his arm as she weaseled herself in between him and Amy. Aaron and Rachel exchanged knowing glances.

Amy's love for sports and the sheer excitement of the rambunctious stadium was obvious as she settled in between Aaron and Rachel with a metal cowbell decorated with streamers and ribbons of their school colors. She rang it loudly and cheered. Aaron leaned over to Cade. "You sure you want to sit this close to us? She gets a bit rowdy." He tossed a thumb over his shoulder toward Amy.

Cade grinned, but before he could answer, Suzanne's shoulder brushed against his other side and had him turning. She began explaining the Friday night football rituals as Coach Eric Stanton climbed his way up the bleachers toward Amy.

Though there was a brief hesitation in Aaron's steps, he made room for the man to stand next to Amy.

"Ms. Frasier is heavily involved with the athletic department," Suzanne explained to him. "Especially the girls' basketball team. I suppose it's because of Coach Stanton. They've had an off and on relationship for years. I'm sure you've heard," she gossiped.

Cade inhaled a deep breath and lightly rubbed a hand over the back of his neck as music began to play and the home team ran through an enormous poster banner, tearing it down the middle and rushing to the sidelines. Amy leaned forward and caught his attention. "Ready for your first football game, Wickerson?"

"Bring it on."

Amy handed him a spare cowbell and flashed a quick grin before cheering loudly with the cheerleaders. When their team kicked off, a loud roar vibrated through the bleachers and Cade found his surrounding teachers to be fun, enthusiastic, and supportive of their students. They knew every name of every player and even some of the parents that sat around them. So far, he appreciated the positive camaraderie. Well, from everyone but Suzanne. She wasn't horribly rude, but when a quiet moment hushed over the crowd, that's when she'd take a moment to share some other negative tidbit about Amy in a hushed whisper. So far, Cade wasn't impressed with her tactics.

The first quarter had drifted by quickly, the Bulldogs trailing by one touchdown, but the second quarter picked up speed and they now led the opposing visitors by seven points. When the buzzer sounded for halftime, Amy stood and stretched her legs. She reached for her cell phone, glancing down at the screen and seeing a notification for a voicemail. She looked up at her friends. "Gotta go get some grub. I'll be back." She sidestepped down the aisle of the bleachers and accidentally stepped on Cade's foot in the process. "Oops! Sorry, Wickerson." He gently grabbed her elbow to help her regain her balance. "Are you leaving?"

"Nope. I have to satisfy my halftime munchies. I'll be back in a few." She avoided Suzanne's gaze as she passed by and headed down the stairs toward the main riser and to the ground.

"Excuse me." Cade held up a finger to ward off Suzanne's conversation, more pointless gossip about other teachers, and stepped around her. He hurried after Amy, catching up to her as she spoke with a couple sporting school colors, the woman with a painted #32 on her right cheek. Cade hesitated a moment, the woman's eyes briefly glancing over Amy's shoulder causing Amy to turn and see who'd stepped up. Her face split into a welcoming smile. "This is our newest recruit to the high school," she introduced. "Cade Wickerson. He teaches Ryan in English class."

The proud parents of the pizza delivery boy shook his hand in greeting. "Ryan told us he has become friends with your nephew, Rilan," the man stated. "He seems to think they'll be good friends."

"I hope so. I've enjoyed having Ryan in class this week." Cade gave an affirmative nod and the parents waved at another couple making their way to the bathrooms and concession stand. Amy waved them onward as she hung back to talk with Cade. "They seem like nice people."

"They are," Amy said, with a pleased smile on her face. "You'll find most of the parents here are pretty involved with their kids' schooling. It's one of the reasons I like teaching here." She looked up at him. "So, what brings you down the bleachers?"

Not wanting to shed light on the fact he wanted to visit with her, he pointed to concessions. "I could use a drink."

"Oh, you should have told me. I could have brought one back."

"I needed to stretch my legs a bit."

"Me too. Plus, I gotta get my halftime nachos. If I don't, we might lose."

He laughed at her statement. "Is that so? You're not superstitious are you, Frazzle?"

She held up her thumb and pointer finger an inch apart. "Every time I eat nachos, they win. The few times I've skipped out, they've lost. So, now it's sort of a thing. The kids expect me to eat nachos."

"So, they'll be watching?"

"For sure."

"Sounds like a lot of pressure."

She shrugged on an exaggerated sigh. "A burden I'm willing to carry, especially when they come with extra jalapenos."

He laughed. "Now you're just making me hungry."

"There's nothing better than concession stand nachos, Wickerson. Do yourself a favor and splurge."

"But what if I throw off your mojo? What if you're the only one that can eat nachos?"

"Good point." She rubbed her chin. "Well, we have to at least test the theory that your nacho craving won't throw off the game. What better time than the first game of the season? We have all season to make up for a loss."

Chuckling, he slid his hands into his pockets as they stepped in line for the concession stand.

"Besides, where else can you find $1.50 nachos in town?"

"You've brought up some good points." They reached the counter and Amy ordered her nachos while Cade held up two fingers for the volunteer parent to go ahead and double it. He fished in his wallet for some bills and as two loaded down nacho trays landed on the counter, along with a large soda, he handed the woman the money.

"You don't have to buy my food." Amy turned in surprise and he waved away her concern.

"You can get it next time."

"Fair enough." She grabbed two straws for the single soda and popped them in the top. "Red is yours, blue is mine." She pointed to the two colors, and he nodded, appreciative she'd even share. "Let's start back, because it might take a while."

Confused as to why their short walk would become a journey, Cade fell into step beside her. Amy popped a chip into her mouth and closed her eyes. "The first bite of the year. Glorious."

He laughed and took a bite of his own, relishing in the same nostalgic flavors.

"Good, right?" She waited for his nod of agreement before pointing toward the stands. "So, your first week of school flew by. You're liked by the kids. You're liked by the staff. How do you feel about the school?"

"I like it." A couple of teenagers paused a moment to talk to Amy, commented on her nachos, gave her enthusiastic high fives for her consistency and support, and then darted away. "So far it feels like a good fit."

"I think it is too. I like having you across the hall."

"Thanks. You're not so bad a neighbor yourself, despite what Suzanne says."

Amy scoffed and then smirked. "I'm glad you think so. And when it comes to what Suzanne says about me, I hope you'll come to me if she ever says anything that might be… I don't know… questionable. She doesn't really like me, nor does she truly know me. And though I don't know what all she says about me, I'm sure some of it may be a bit… exaggerated."

"Don't worry. I take everything she says with a grain of salt."

"I knew you were a smart one." Amy stopped in her tracks again as several students emerged and began speaking with both of them. And Amy had been right; their trek back to the bleachers took them well into the third quarter because of how many times students and parents wanted to stop and chat with her. He liked that she was well-liked by everyone, further proving Suzanne's disdain for her was an uncommon response. Amy greeted everyone warmly, gave them attention and focus, and introduced him to everyone that stopped them. She was open and welcoming, and her vibrant personality left people with smiles. So far, Cade only wanted to know her better. He watched her rake her finger through the leftover cheese of her empty nacho container before tossing it in the trash, and as she stuck her finger in her lips to finish off the tasty meal, she froze. "I have to eat it all. Tradition, you know."

Laughing, Cade tossed his empty container in the garbage as well. Amy reached into her purse and pulled out a wet wipe for herself and one for him to wipe their hands. When they'd finished, she handed him the soda and he took a long sip before handing it back to her. "Now, let's go win a football game." She slapped a hearty pat on his back and grinned as she rushed up the bleachers to their seats. Both Eric and Suzanne did not seem pleased to see them arrive together, and Cade caught the amused expression from Aaron at their shared soda as Amy began cheering loudly for the team.

∞

"That's two clean canastas for me now." Amy stacked her row of sevens into a neat pile and nudged them to the side. "And I discard a black three." She placed her card on the center pile and watched as James leaned forward to survey the rows of cards in front of him. "You're very good at this, Amy."

"Thanks. I had a good teacher." His eyes sparkled at her comment as he drew two cards from the center pile to start his turn. "Have you talked with Peter this week?"

"I haven't." Amy watched as he shifted and sorted the cards in his hand and then discarded, bringing the game back to her. "The last I heard from him he said he was heading here later today. Is that right?"

"Yes. He is. He's a good boy. Takes good care of me. Just like Lucille." He nodded over his shoulder to the nurse that sat at a nearby table playing checkers with another resident of the assisted living home. "And I like that you came to see me. I don't get many visitors. Just Peter."

"Well, now that I know you live so close, we'll have to make this a regular thing." Amy drew two pointless cards and nibbled her bottom lip before deciding to discard a four.

"I've got you penciled in for dinner when Peter is in town. I already told him."

"I'm glad." Amy waved for him to take his turn and watched as he began laying card after card and creating the needed combinations to go out and stick her with points against her. He held up his hands with a magician's flourish and she laughed. "You got me again."

"You're still learning, so I can't take too much credit." James began reshuffling the cards and Amy briefly glanced at her watch. They'd made it the entire round with him mentally staying in the present. She saw his hands hesitate a moment as if forgetting what movement was needed to bring the cards together. His eyes, clouded and uncertain, looked up at Amy. "Becca?"

She forced a bright smile. "Hi, James."

"Well, what are you doing here? I thought you were in Cincinnati this week?"

"Why would I be in Cincinnati?"

"You told me last week you were performing in Cincinnati for the fair."

"Oh, right." Amy smiled. "Well, I'm not in Cincinnati, James. I'm here with you. What do you say, can I beat you at cards today?"

He laughed and squeezed her hand that rested on the table, his eyes hovering a moment over his aged fingers compared to her youthful ones. Confusion furrowed his brow. "The oddest thing." He whispered. "It's like you're a dream, Becca. Just a dream."

Sadness flooded Amy's heart as she squeezed his hand. "Why don't you take a rest, James? We can play later."

His eyes darted around the room and landed upon Lucille, his eyes sparking with recognition for one fleeting moment. His voice, tired now, drifted from his chair. "I think I will, my heart's love. I think I will."

Amy caught Lucille's eye and the woman hopped to her feet and hurried over. "Mr. James, you ready for a rest now?"

"Yes, Lucy, I am. Becca came to see me."

"I see that." Lucille, not even glancing Amy's direction helped him situate from the chair at the table back into his wheelchair.

"She's good about coming to see me, isn't she?" James continued.

"Always lovely to see Ms. Becca," Lucille agreed. "Now, let's get you on down to your room." She nodded a farewell to Amy as they rounded the corner.

Amy sighed, wishing she could stay and continue their card game. She noticed the resident at the checkers game continued to play even without Lucille's presence. She then noticed several other residents quietly building puzzles, reading books, playing games, or watching television by themselves. They didn't have any company. An idea sparked and Amy reached for her cell phone on her way out the door. Texting Rachel, she pitched a new idea for their Student Council kids. Volunteering at the assisted living home would be great community service hours for the students, and she couldn't think of a better opportunity than for the students to get to know the older generations. Her phone buzzed with Rachel's excited response to the idea and already making notes to pitch it to the principal. A text message popped up on her screen from Peter, thanking her for visiting James and finalizing dinner plans for later in the evening. It'd be nice to see him again. And time with James was refreshing to her. His love for Becca was overwhelmingly sweet, and though Amy hated the fact that the man had lost his wife, she loved that she could bring back positive feelings and memories for him when his mind wasn't so clear. A love like that should be remembered.

She opened her car door and tossed her purse over onto the passenger seat before climbing inside behind the wheel. Glancing at the clock, she realized she had just enough time to drive home, shower, dress, and be ready for Peter to swing by to pick her up for dinner by six. The drive was short, and Rachel awaited her on her front porch, as though she knew Amy needed a female presence to help decide what to wear.

"You seem in a rush," Rachel acknowledged as Amy hurried into her house.

"I only have about an hour or so before Peter comes to pick me up."

"Peter? As in the guy from the other night at Romero's?"

"Yes. I'm eating with him and James tonight. Make yourself at home, I'll be out in a few minutes." Amy darted to the shower, making quick work of washing her hair.

Rachel sat with her arms crossed as Amy rushed about the house looking for random articles of clothing and accessories. She stumbled into the living room, slipping on a pair of plum high heels. "Anyway, I was hoping for you guys to meet Peter, so I told him to pick me up at Aaron's house. Want to dart over there with me?"

Rachel eyed Amy's outfit. "That's what you're wearing? That's a pretty dress. Is it new?" Rachel commented, bringing attention to the fact Amy had changed into a flattering little black dress.

"I bought it a couple of weeks ago. I wasn't sure where we would be eating dinner, so thought I'd better dress up just in case they decided on somewhere nice."

"Is that the only reason?" Rachel teased, taking a sip from Amy's favorite polka dot tea mug.

"Why wouldn't it be?" she asked innocently.

Rachel just shook her head in dismay. "Tell me about Peter. Is he a good-looking guy?"

Amy shrugged. "He's handsome. Really kind."

"And this new little number—" Rachel pointed at Amy's dress. "Is this for him?"

"I told you. I'm not sure what type of restaurant we are eating at. I want to look nice just in case we go somewhere a bit nicer than Romero's. And if you're asking me if I'm interested in Peter, the answer is no."

"That is exactly what I was asking you," Rachel admitted. "And I was just curious because I haven't seen you dress up for anyone in a while."

"Well, technically I'm dressing up for his grandpa."

"Which doesn't sound weird at all," Rachel laughed, and quickly had Amy doing the same.

"I guess it does. I just... if he thinks I'm Becca, I want his moments with her to be special."

"I think you're putting too much pressure on yourself. I mean, he saw you as Abe Lincoln and thought you were her."

"True. Though he said something about a circus, and today he mentioned a fair. I would love to hear why that was his first thought and if maybe she was involved in a circus somehow. The more I learn of her, the more interesting she sounds. I stopped by his assisted living home and played cards with him. Apparently, Becca was quite the card player too." She grabbed her purse and headed toward the door. "Come on, let's head to Aaron's."

CHAPTER ELEVEN

Cade watched as Amy's small black car whipped into Aaron's driveway. Rilan and Cade were currently elbow deep in soil as they planted fresh shrubbery and plants along the front of the house. Rachel hopped out of the car and waved as Amy stepped out. His breath caught at the sight of her.

She wore a simple black dress with a swooping boatneck, a delicate necklace with a single amethyst drop, and heels. Heels that made him focus on the length of her legs longer than he should have, as he felt a clump of dirt hit him against the shoulder and Rilan stood with a smug grin on his face.

Amy spotted them and waved. "Hey guys!"

"Hey yourself." Cade walked up and extended his hand. She accepted it and he twirled her in a quick circle. "And what has you all fancied up?"

She smiled. "James."

"Oh. The old guy?" Rilan asked.

Amy nodded. "Yep. He's my hot date tonight. Well, he and his grandson, Peter," she admitted. "Peter was back in town, so he asked if I would join them." She lightly ran a hand over the tight twist in the back of her hair and smiled as Peter's SUV pulled next to the curb.

"Sounds like a fun night." Cade reached forward, his fingers tickling her skin as he adjusted the clasp of her necklace for her. He shifted it from the front to the back. Her hand grazed up to gently press the purple stone against her skin when he was finished.

"Thanks." Her eyes held his for a moment, and he hated the idea she was to eat with another man that night. "Wish you could join us tonight." Her hazel eyes tugged at him.

"I wouldn't want to come between James and his Becca." He lowered his voice. "You look beautiful."

She blushed. "Thanks. I'm a bit nervous. I don't know why. I guess I just don't want to let James down. Is that weird?"

"No. It's sweet." He brushed his knuckle over her cheek and her eyes flashed back up to his. He quickly lowered his hand.

"I'd love for you to meet him." She reached for his hand and began tugging him forward. His reluctant footsteps had her turning. "What's the matter?"

"Amy, I'm—" He waved a hand over his dirty clothes and arms. "Covered in dirt."

"So? They won't care." She grabbed his hand again and pulled him along behind her as Aaron was already shaking Peter's hand. Amy smiled and gave Peter a light hug. "I hope you don't mind, but I wanted my friends to meet you and James."

"Not at all," Peter smiled warmly. "You look lovely, Amy."

"Thank you. Is James in back?" she asked, pointing to the rear window.

"He is." Peter walked to the car and opened the passenger door. James turned, and a bright smile spread over his worn, but handsome face. "Amy! So good to see you, my girl. My, don't you look beautiful. Doesn't she, Peter?"

"Hi there, James." Thankful that James was himself, she quickly introduced him to her friends.

"So great to meet you all. Amy's a real gem. Why, she brightens this old man's day when she comes to visit."

"Visit?" Aaron asked.

"Why, at the home of course. Beats me in Canasta every time." He reached forward, and Amy clasped his hand. She looked to Cade, and he winked.

"Well, we better get going if we are to have dinner. I'm starving. How about you, James?"

"Oh, most definitely. We're going to one of my favorite places."

"Is that so?" Amy grinned at Peter.

"Peter, well he—" James paused a moment, his eyes slightly narrowing as he studied Peter. "Bill? Bill, why are we in the car? Where are we going?"

They saw Peter's shoulders fall a bit as he closed the car door and rolled down his grandfather's window. "It's me, Grandpa. Peter. Bill's son. We're going to dinner."

"Oh, how nice." James looked to everyone else and when his eyes landed on Amy he gasped. "Becca! My heart!" He reached for her, and Amy stepped forward and clasped his hand once again in hers.

"Hi, James." She kissed his cheek. "Let's go to dinner." She stepped away from the car and Peter rolled up the window. He shook everyone's hands again.

"Sorry about that, he's in out and these days. Amy's been a real blessing to him. To both of us, really."

Amy waved his comment away. "He's wonderful." She looked to her friends and smiled. "I'll see you guys later. Aaron, mind if I have them drop me off here when we're done?"

"That's fine. If Rachel takes your car somewhere, I can drive you home."

"I can do that," Cade quickly offered and then cleared his throat. "If... if that's alright?"

Amy's eyes shined as she nodded. "I'd like that." She nodded in approval at the idea and then walked around to the passenger side, Peter opening her door for her. She waved at Rilan before hopping inside.

When they drove away, Aaron shoved Cade. "What was that about?"

Cade's face betrayed him, and Rachel excitedly clapped her hands. He held up a hand to ward off her reaction, which just made Aaron laugh.

"Caaade!" Rachel squealed.

"It's not like that. I just want to hear about her time with James. I find his story interesting. That is all."

"Are you sure?" Aaron asked, pointing to Rilan behind him mocking his uncle.

Cade grabbed his nephew and tucked him under his sweaty arm in the crook of his elbow and began rubbing his knuckles in his hair. "All of you can just stop now. I'm going back to dig some dirt."

Rilan raised his head on a laugh. "Five bucks says he's showered and cleaned up before Amy gets home so he can walk her home looking fresh."

"I don't make bets I know I will lose," Aaron continued teasing as Cade made his way back to his shovel, completely ignoring them. But he felt the truth of their words and hated that he was so transparent. When did he lose himself to Amy? When did his wanting to be friends with her officially cross the line into something more? It was James. James had done it. When she talked of James kissing her and thinking she was his wife, Becca, Cade had fallen. The love she had for a perfect stranger. The hope she wished to bring an old man with kind words and the joy of seeing his beloved wife even for a split-second melted Cade's heart. The fact that Amy had visited the man at his retirement facility just to brighten his day spoke volumes as to the type of woman she was. But he still barely knew her, and that weight fell upon his shoulders as he thought of Rilan. He'd need to be cautious. With anyone he'd dated in the past, he always made sure Rilan was his main priority. Those relationships never worked out, because most could not understand or fully welcome a teenager into their life as well as Cade. He understood. It was a unique situation. But he hoped, and felt, that perhaps Amy was a woman who could. Time would tell. But before he could even think of confessions of love and grand gestures, he had to build more of a foundation with her. And that is what he hoped to accomplish when she came home.

He tapped his shoe against the shovel, digging deeper into the moist earth and tossing the dirt aside as he felt Rilan's studious gaze. Cade needed to guard his feelings toward Amy. If his nephew saw through him, then other students might as well. And the last thing he wanted was to be the new teacher making puppy dog eyes to the teacher across the hall. When Rilan went back to digging, he thanked the stars his nephew didn't push it any further.

∞

Peter paid for their meal and thanked the waitress before she walked away. Amy took a long sip of her wine and smiled lovingly at James as he snoozed next to the table.

"Thank you again, Amy, for joining us. And for visiting him at the retirement center. It was the first thing he told me about when I arrived."

"It was nothing. He's sweet. And I will admit, I find his stories fascinating. Your grandmother sounded like an incredible lady."

"She was," Peter agreed. "I've always hoped I'd find a love like they had."

"I think anyone would want to," Amy admitted.

"Speaking of—" Peter prodded. "The man you introduced me to— Cade, I believe his name was— is that your boyfriend?"

Amy's shoulders straightened. "No. Why would you think that?"

Peter chuckled. "Just seemed you two had a connection."

"Oh." Her eyes wandered a moment and he grinned.

"I don't mean to pry, Amy. It's none of my business," Peter apologized.

"No, it's fine. It's just... Cade's just a friend. He's new in town and teaches across the hall from me, so we've become friends."

"I see."

"I mean, not *good* friends. Not yet, anyway. School's only been in session for a week, so it's not like much could really happen in that time frame." She babbled on and Peter eased back into his chair and patiently sipped on the remains of his drink as he listened with a small smile on his face as her hands waved as she spoke. "And he has his nephew to think of as well, which I'm sure is a lot. But he's great. Cade, I mean. Well, his nephew is sweet too," she amended. "And you know, we'll just have to see how the school year goes." She trailed off and then noticed Peter's amused expression. "And you didn't need to know all of that." She laughed and covered her face in mortification as he laughed.

"Don't be embarrassed." Peter reached over and patted her hand. "I'm actually going through something quite similar at the moment."

"Really?" Amy's brows rose.

"Yes, though cross country. Amanda lives in New York. And well, I'm in San Francisco. Grandpa is here in Texas. Makes for some complications."

"Wow, yeah..." Amy sighed. "And here I am worried about the man across the hall."

Peter chuckled.

"So, what about your parents? Can they not see to James?"

"Unfortunately, no. My father passed away several years ago and my mother lives in Florida. James is my father's dad, so my mother, short of checking on him every now and then, isn't as dedicated to his care as she is to her own parents who live with her in Florida."

"Which is quite a bit of responsibility already, I imagine," Amy added.

"Right. And I'm the only grandchild. He's not a burden, mind you, it's just hard to fly out as often as I would like. I've thought about moving him to San Fran, but the retirement home he's at here is much better than any I've found there. Plus, I hate to take him away from what little he still recognizes. He's had the same caretaker for years,

Lucille. Bless her. I'm afraid too much of a change would be hard for him."

"Well, I don't mind checking up on him every now and then if you can't make it to town. I know you barely know me, but I'm willing to help."

"I appreciate you. Just since seeing you the first time, the nurses say he's been more lucid, but also that his attitude has improved. He was feeling quite low for a while, and you've lit a spark in him."

"He loved Becca so much. It's honestly astounding to see. I've never seen anything like it."

"They were high school sweethearts. Actually, more like childhood sweethearts. They met when they were seven. Grandpa told everyone he would marry that Becca girl someday. And he did."

Amy held a hand to her heart and cast a tender gaze at a snoring James. "That's incredible."

"He called her his 'Heart's Love.' Saying his heart knew it loved her even before he did. So, from then on, Heart's Love, was what he called her. The rest of us in the family just called her Lovie."

"That's cute," Amy grinned. "Heart's Love. I like that too."

Peter shrugged as though epic love stories were an everyday occurrence. "Anyway, I hate to cut this evening off, but—" He pointed at James.

"Yes. He would be more comfortable out of that chair." Amy stood and waited as Peter unlocked the brakes on James's chair wheels and began rolling him toward the exit. "Thank you for this evening, Peter. It was a breath of fresh air."

"I'm glad." He loaded a groggy James into the back seat and then opened Amy's door for her. "To your friend's house?"

"Yes, please. Cade is walking me home."

"Ah, is he?" Peter's brow rose as he smiled.

Amy fidgeted by rubbing a hand over the skirt of her dress. "Yes. And don't."

"Don't what?" Peter asked.

"Don't look at me like that." She smirked as he laughed.

"Well, I wish you a wonderful walk." Peter pulled the car against the curb. Amy's car was gone, which meant Rachel either dropped it off at Amy's house and grabbed her own car, or that Aaron and Rachel took it somewhere. Cade's front porch light was on, but his house sat still, his flower beds neatly planted. "Would you like me to wait?"

"If you don't mind?"

"Not at all."

Amy hopped out of the vehicle casting one more glance toward James's sleeping form. "Tell him good night for me?"

"Will do," Peter promised. "Now go ring his doorbell."

Amy flushed and Peter nodded in the direction of Cade's house. "Go."

She inhaled a deep breath and smiled. "I'm going, bossy pants," she muttered, hearing his soft laugh as she walked up the walkway to Cade's front door. She hesitated for one second and then pressed the button.

∞

Cade and Rilan sat on the couch, their feet propped on the coffee table, bowls of cereal in their hands as they watched the latest in the line of superhero films. The surround sound reverberated around the room and had Cade surprised when he heard the soft chime of the doorbell.

"Probably Amy." Rilan, his eyes never leaving the screen, mouthed another spoonful of cereal. Cade's lips twitched as he watched his nephew a moment longer before heading toward the door. He opened it to find Amy nervously winding her hands together.

"Hey," she greeted, a tenuous smile on her face.

"Hey."

"Still up for that walk?"

He looked down at his half eaten cereal bowl before setting it on the entry table. "Of course."

"Oh." She looked at his bowl. "You can finish eating. I didn't mean to—"

"No, it's fine." Cade began to step out as Amy turned and offered a farewell wave to Peter. Cade did as well, and they both watched as the silver SUV made its way up the street. "How was your dinner?"

A soft smile tugged at her lips. "It was wonderful."

"I'm glad."

"Your plants look nice."

"Thanks. I'm afraid my back's a bit sore from digging holes, but it at least looks a bit more landscaped now."

"Oh, well if your back is bothering you, I don't want you to feel like you have to walk me home." Sympathy marred her features, and he waved it away.

"I'm good. Trust me, if it were that bad, I wouldn't have been able to make it off the couch."

"Well, I appreciate it. However, I will admit," Amy paused and gripped his forearm as she stood on one foot and grabbed the high heel off the other. She then switched feet and removed the other shoe as well. "These have been killing my feet, and I can't imagine walking home in them."

Cade chuckled. "I could drive you."

"And miss this beautiful weather? It's not every day a girl gets fed a lovely meal by two handsome men and then has the privilege of a moonlight stroll with another one. Let me revel in this moment."

Laughing, Cade waved her onward. Her hand never left his arm, but instead she linked it through his as they walked.

"Becca, turns out, met James when they were seven years old."

"Really?" Cade asked, intrigued.

"Yes. And apparently James professed his love for her then and swore he'd marry her."

"Which he obviously did," Cade finished.

"He did." Amy sighed happily. "Can you imagine a love like that? Peter and I were discussing it, and it just seems so extraordinary."

Cade contemplated her question. "I think that love can hit someone at any moment. Though I sometimes doubt it being possible in my own life, I don't doubt it happens to other people."

"See, I feel the same way. But hearing James, and even Peter, talking about Becca and their relationship... it's so uplifting. He called her his 'Heart's Love,' and everyone called her Lovie because of it. I mean, could you get any more precious?"

Cade grinned at her excitement. "That *is* pretty cute."

"*Right?* Anyway, it was an awesome evening, and I'm glad I get to finish it by talking with you. So, did you do anything fun today? Or just work outside?"

"Rilan and I played some basketball in the midst of our planting sessions."

"Why didn't he try out for the team?"

"Still trying to get his feet wet, I guess."

"And how was your first football game experience? I haven't had a chance to ask you about it since we won."

"It was fun. And I will admit that once the game started, Suzanne was not as obnoxious as I anticipated."

"Really?" Amy asked, impressed. "I'm glad."

"Yeah. I mean, she sort of started out a little…" He grimaced. "But then she seemed to warm up toward the end of the game. She asked me to dinner tomorrow night," he mentioned and felt Amy slightly tense at his words.

"Wow. Where are you guys going?"

"Not sure yet. I told her I would have to let her know if I can. I hadn't talked to Rilan about it yet."

"And have you talked to him about it since?"

"No, actually." He rubbed a hand over the back of his neck.

"Dreading that, I see. He's got to know you date, Cade," Amy teased. "I'm sure he'll be fine knowing his uncle is going out on a date."

"I'm not so sure."

"Why wouldn't he be?"

"He's rather opinionated when it comes to women."

Amy laughed. "You know, I could see that."

Cade grinned. "Besides, I'm just not sure I want to go."

"Suzanne knows where you live, she will more than likely show up to pick you up tomorrow if you don't call her beforehand and let her know you don't want to go. Unless you do decide to go, and then you won't have to call her because she'll just show up to pick you up." Amy giggled as he lightly elbowed her in the side.

Cade slowed his pace as they rounded the corner of Amy's street and her house came into view. The walk was too short for his liking, and he wasn't quite ready to relinquish his time with her. She matched his pace, as though she wanted to prolong their time together as well. He wasn't sure how Amy felt about him really. He felt her reaction when he mentioned Suzanne, but she seemed somewhat supportive of the idea. Or she was playing it cool. He just couldn't tell. And he wasn't interested in Suzanne, but he did admit it would be nice to get his own feet wet again. He hadn't dated anyone for quite some time, and he feared he might be a bit rusty.

"Well, here we are." Amy stopped at the end of her sidewalk and gazed at her small house. "Home sweet home." She smiled up at him as he led her to the porch. Her car sat parked in the driveway for her. "Thanks for walking me back."

"My pleasure." She reluctantly slipped her arm from his and unlocked her door. She turned and he soaked in one last, long look of her all dressed up. "You really do look beautiful tonight. Bare feet and all."

Her teeth flashed in a dazzling smile as she did a small spin. "Why thank you, Mr. Wickerson." She curtsied. "Maybe I will see you tomorrow before your big date," she winked.

He stuffed his hands in his pockets. "I don't know if I will clean up half as good as you, but I'll do my best."

Laughing, Amy rubbed a hand over her chin. "Yes, well, I did have to shave my beard and lose my top hat." She then changed her tone of voice to her Abraham Lincoln impersonation. "Oh, the things we do for love."

He shook his head at her antics and tried not to laugh but failed. "Goodnight, Abe."

"Goodnight, my heart's love," she teased, winking at him as she slipped inside her house and shut the door.

Eyeing her house a moment longer, Cade looked up to the night's sky and stared at the stars a moment. Heart's love. A simple phrase that sounded like it bounced right off the pages of Shakespeare or Chaucer. A simple endearment that registered depth and feeling. And though he knew she used it lightheartedly, Cade found himself almost wishing he could be the man to sweep her off her feet like James did Becca. Time would tell. But first, he needed to jump back into the dating game and work out the kinks. Perhaps a date with Suzanne would do just that.

CHAPTER TWELVE

"I still can't believe he said yes." Aaron looked to Rachel for explanation, and she shrugged her shoulders.

"He said she wasn't that bad," Amy explained. "Maybe he wants to see that side of her a bit more to gauge whether or not he wants to pursue her."

"And you're okay with this?"

"What kind of question is that?" Amy asked on a laugh as she walked over to Aaron's couch and plopped down into her favorite corner of the cushions.

Rachel crossed her arms and leaned against the chair Aaron sat in. "Suzanne? And you don't have a single negative comment?"

"Maybe she's turning over a new leaf," Amy defended.

"Right. *Or* she's just hitting on the newest eligible bachelor," Rachel added.

"Why does it bother you so bad?" Aaron asked.

"Because it is *Suzanne.*" Rachel held up her hands as though the other two were not getting it. "And as Cade's friend, are we not supposed to look out for him?"

Aaron laughed. "He's a grown man. Besides, I don't think he's planning on a serious relationship with her. He's new here and she's a friendly face wanting to get to know him."

"And what if they hit it off and start dating? Suzanne hates us," Rachel reminded Amy.

"She doesn't hate us," Amy corrected. "She dislikes us. There's a difference."

"Right." Rachel rolled her eyes and held a hand to her stomach as it growled.

"Easy, tiger," Aaron teased.

"I'm starving. Are we going to go eat somewhere?"

"Romero's?" Aaron asked.

"I could go for some Romero's." Amy stood and slipped her shoes on. "I could use a big glass of wine and lasagna."

"Please stop talking about food." Rachel's stomach rumbled again as Aaron shooed them toward his truck. Amy hopped in the front seat as Rachel slid in the back. "Should we check on Rilan?"

"He's sixteen." Amy shook her head. "Besides, if Cade wanted you to play babysitter, he would have asked."

"I'm not trying to babysit. I just didn't know if Aaron had agreed to keep an eye on him while Cade was out."

"Nope. He didn't ask."

"Then there we go." Amy leaned her head back against the headrest until Aaron turned into the parking lot of Romero's and found a spot toward the front. The inviting aromas of fresh baked bread sticks had her mouth watering and her stomach echoing Rachel's sentiments from earlier. They walked to their usual booth and sat, offering friendly waves to some of the wait staff that recognized them as regulars. Rachel squeezed into the booth next to Amy, squishing her up against the wall as she tried to arrange their purses in the seat as well. She finally gave up and handed them over the table to Aaron to fit on his side so she and Rachel could eat without bumping elbows.

Their favorite waiter, Timothy, walked up with a dazzling white smile against dark skin, his charm aimed, as always, at Rachel. Timothy helped manage the restaurant while also attending night classes to earn his doctorate in computer science. Amy liked him. He was fun, charming, easy on the eyes, and smart. She wasn't quite sure why Rachel hadn't pursued that flirtation yet.

"What will it be guys?" He stood, hands behind his back expectantly, no pen or pad, because his mind worked like a steel trap. With all the research he had to do for school, Amy figured he was just used to memorizing things, and food orders were effortless for him.

"Pinot Grigio and lasagna for me," Amy told him.

He looked to Rachel. "Caesar salad, manicotti, and same wine, please." He smiled and nodded before turning to Aaron.

"I'll have what Ames is having, but with the house red, Tim. Thanks."

"No problem. I'll have it out shortly." He buzzed away and returned a few short minutes later with their drinks before expertly disappearing again and checking up on his other assigned tables.

Amy took the first chilled sip of the crisp white wine and swished it around inside her mouth. Delicious. She held her glass to her lips to sip some more, but Rachel grabbed her arm and softly gasped. "Look." She nodded toward the center of the room.

Amy and Aaron leaned forward and turned their heads only to find Cade and Suzanne sitting at one of the center tables.

Suzanne looked beautiful; classy with her blond hair perfectly styled around her shoulders. Her makeup was pristine, as well as the white dress she wore. And Cade... well, Amy had to admit he looked just as becoming. Though she could see tension in his posture, he seemed relaxed enough that he offered a casual smile to whatever Suzanne was talking about. She felt bad for staring and turned back to her wine. "At least Suzanne has good taste in restaurants," Amy pointed out.

"That she does," Aaron agreed. "I wonder what they're talking about."

"It's none of our business," Amy warned him as she tapped Rachel's arm to make sure her friend had stopped staring at them as well.

"I'm curious too," Rachel admitted in a whisper. "Oh, look. Tim's their waiter too. Maybe he can tell us."

"Guys." Amy narrowed her gaze at them. "Please, act like mature adults."

"I can't help it. I've never seen Suzanne act so normal," Aaron stated. "It's like watching a tiger trying to appear like a house cat. I can't look away for fear of missing when her true nature strikes."

Amy couldn't help the laugh that bubbled forth and she tossed a piece of a breadstick at him that he caught in his mouth. Her head tilted in an impressed nod before she shook her head at his distraction toward the other table.

Timothy walked up and blocked their view, both Rachel and Aaron leaning around him to keep staring. Timothy turned to see what caught their eye. "Did you guys want their attention?" he asked.

"No." Rachel placed a hand on Timothy's arm as she whispered. "He's our friend. And she's our coworker... that we don't really like."

"Ah. I see." He placed their silverware and napkins on the table. "Anything else I can get you guys?"

"What are they talking about?" Rachel asked.

Amy popped her friend with her cloth napkin and Rachel squealed in protest, several people turning to look, including Cade and Suzanne. Timothy and Aaron laughed as Rachel rubbed her arm. "That hurt, Ames."

"It was meant to. Stop being rude. We're fine, Tim. Thanks." He grinned as he darted away.

Cade offered a brief wave to the table and Aaron answered it. "Well, we've been spotted," he whispered.

"That's fine. Let them continue their evening. We have our own meals to eat." Amy forked a mouthful of lasagna and closed her eyes as she relished the flavors she'd been craving since stepping in the door. When she opened her eyes, Cade was standing by their table.

∞

"Hey guys," he greeted, sliding into the seat next to Aaron. Both women shot a glance at his table and noticed Suzanne had disappeared. "She went to freshen up."

"So, how's it going?" Aaron asked.

"Okay, I guess. Hasn't been too bad," Cade admitted. He watched as Amy avoided eye contact and continued to eat her meal. "I didn't realize you guys were coming here tonight. We could have made it a group date."

"Trust me, this is for the best." Rachel pointed at the two separate tables and Cade laughed at her honesty.

"Hey there, Amy." He wanted her to look at him, and he was a bit unsure as to why she hadn't. She looked up and forced a polite smile before taking a long sip of her wine.

"Hey, I'll be right back." Rachel smiled as she waved to someone across the restaurant. "I see a girl from spin class." She hurried across the room and eased into a vacant chair to chat with her friend.

"You guys plan to be here for a bit?" Cade asked.

"Probably another hour," Aaron answered. "Why?"

"Mind if I hitch a ride back with you guys?"

Amy's brows rose at his statement, but she didn't utter a word.

"That bad, huh?" Aaron chuckled.

"Oh, no. It's just we are pretty much wrapping things up, and I would like to hang out with you guys. It would save Suzanne the trip too."

"That's fine," Aaron told him. He pointed. "And there she awaits you."

Cade turned to see Suzanne making her way back to their table, a fresh coat of lipstick on her flawless smile. Cade tapped his knuckles on the table as he walked toward her and explained his new plans to stick around. Amy avoided watching.

"She doesn't look too happy," Aaron reported. "Probably upset she won't get that end of date kiss."

"Oh Lord, would you stop? You're as bad as Rachel."

"What? She probably is. I would be."

"What?" Amy giggled, and Aaron lowered his head at his blunder.

"I meant, after a date. *Not* after a date with Cade."

Amy burst into laughter again at his expense and wriggled her eyebrows when Cade walked back to their table and sat beside him. Aaron just shook his head in dismay.

"What'd I miss?" Cade asked, glad to finally see Amy back to her cheerful self.

"Aaron was just telling me how disappointed he was going to be if he didn't get an end of date kiss."

Surprised, Cade turned to Aaron. "And which one do you plan on kissing? Amy or Rachel?"

"Or you?" Amy snickered as she took a sip of her drink and Aaron just rolled his eyes.

"Laugh it up, Ames. And the answer is none of you," Aaron clarified. "Absolutely none of you."

"That's a shame," Amy continued. "I would have paid to see you try at least one kiss."

It was his turn to chunk a piece of bread in her direction.

Amy tried to catch it, but the bread bypassed her. "Where'd it go?" She turned her head and looked over her shoulders but didn't see it. She then looked around her lap and Rachel's seat, but still could not find it.

Cade slipped from Aaron's side of the booth and slid next to Amy. Her eyes widened at his close proximity as he reached up and lightly plucked the bread from her hair and held her gaze a moment longer. "Thanks." She plucked the bread from his fingers and tossed it back at Aaron.

Rachel sat next to Aaron when she came back to the table.

"Oh, here Rachel, I'll move. I was just—"

"Nope. You stay there. I'm fine here." She smiled as she pulled her plate towards her and sent a mischievous wink to Amy.

"So how was Suzanne?" Rachel asked.

"Umm... good. I guess. It was good."

"Plan on seeing her again?"

Cade flushed at her rapid-fire questions, but Rachel waited for him to answer. "Not sure. Haven't thought about it."

"You just sat with her for over an hour and you haven't thought about whether or not you would want to again?" Baffled, Rachel forked a piece of salad.

"I mean, yeah, I've considered it. I just haven't made up my mind yet."

"How did Rilan feel about your plans tonight?"

"Whoa, Rachel! None of your business," Amy interrupted. She placed a comforting hand on Cade's arm. "You don't have to answer that. Or any of her questions for that matter. Rachel can be a little *too* nosy at times."

Cade shrugged. "I don't mind." He flashed a friendly smile at Rachel. "And the answer is, he was not happy."

"Why not?" Rachel continued in her interrogation.

"He has his own opinions on who I should date and when."

"I see." Rachel darted her eyes to Amy as her friend sat quietly talking with Aaron, unaware of her inadvertent presence in their conversation.

Cade nodded that Rachel guessed correctly and he tried not to smile at the excitement he saw brighten her face. "Let's not get into that tonight, hm?"

She ran her fingers over her lips as if zipping them up. "For what it's worth, Rilan and I have the same idea." She grinned and drummed her fingers together as if in plotting her next evil move.

Cade cleared his throat as Timothy walked up with a tray of empty glasses. He retrieved Aaron's and placed it with the others. "Dessert?"

"To go, please." Amy looked up at him. "You know what I like."

"The triple chocolate cake it is." Timothy looked to Rachel.

"I think I'm good for tonight. No dessert for me."

He walked off.

"You sure you don't want some *chocolate*?" Amy asked and nodded toward Timothy.

"Oh hush, Ames." She blushed and waved away Amy's comment.

"I saw you checking him out earlier when he passed by, just like you did Aaron at the house party."

Both Aaron and Rachel sputtered at her blunt report. Amy laughed and looked to Cade and nodded. "It happened. I swear." She held up her hand in a scout's honor.

"You are evil." Rachel shook her head as Timothy started walking toward them. "And not a word. Not a word, Ames. Heeeeeeyyy." Rachel flicked her hair over her shoulder as Timothy approached the table again. "So, Timothy, how are your classes this semester?"

His handsome face split into a pleased smile that she would ask, and he began his discourse over what his current schedule looked like. Amy noted he pointed out his free days during the week as if subtly dropping a hint to Rachel that he was indeed available, should she want to call him up sometime. To Amy's surprise, Rachel scribbled her number down on a napkin and handed it to him. "I'm no genius when it comes to computers, but—"

"She's excellent in chemistry." Amy exaggerated her wink at Timothy, and he laughed as Rachel just shook her head in dismay and turned back to him with an embarrassed smile. He pocketed her number and scurried away to grab Amy's cake.

"Chemistry. Ha. Well played, Ames." Aaron fist bumped Amy across the table, and she smiled smugly at Rachel. "Now... what's this about you checking me out?" He turned, batting his lashes at Rachel and she face palmed him, shoving him away. "I am ready to leave," she announced. "Cade, please tell me you have had enough of these lunatics as well."

Cade just snickered as Timothy buzzed by the table and handed Amy her cake. She shouted a thanks as he hurriedly carried a hot tray of food to another one of his tables. She held up the small white Styrofoam container and eyed Cade over the top of it. "You haven't lived, Wickerson, until you've had a piece of Romero's triple chocolate cake."

"Is that so?" He leaned toward her, and his lopsided grin had her pulse jumping. "Then perhaps I might steal a bite of yours."

She tugged the container closer to her as if protecting it. "Sure, but you have to wait until we get home." She lightly shoved his shoulder, so he'd scoot out of the booth. He complied and held a hand down to her to help her to her feet. "Thanks." She led the way to the door as the others followed.

"Shotgun," Rachel called.

Amy's hand had already rested on the front passenger door handle, but she simply took a step further down and waited at the rear door until Aaron unlocked his truck. Cade stood behind her and when the locks clicked, he reached forward, his hand over hers, until she relinquished her hold, and he opened her door. "You didn't have to do that," she muttered as she climbed into the backseat. Shrugging, he closed her door and made his way to the other side and hopped inside.

∞

Rilan sat on the porch of Cade's house when they pulled into Aaron's driveway. Amy waved cheerfully at him as she stepped out of the truck and then waited as Cade rounded the back end. Rilan's brows rose in surprise at seeing his uncle with them when he'd left earlier with Suzanne. He smiled and stood, walking over to them. "Where'd you find this loser?" He tossed a thumb toward Cade before lightly punching him. "The date not end well, Uncle Cade?"

"Date was fine," he replied. "Just bumped into these guys and hitched a ride. You waiting up for me? Did I miss curfew?" Cade teased.

"Almost." Rilan pretended to glance at a watch on his wrist. "I was just on the phone and decided to sit outside."

"Kind of late for a phone call." Cade eyed his nephew curiously. "A girl?"

"No, Ryan. He was hitting me up for basketball at the park tomorrow."

"Ah." Cade reached over and shook Aaron's hand. "Thanks for the ride."

"Anytime."

Rachel and Aaron walked toward his house and Amy followed Cade. Rilan pointed over Cade's shoulder, and he stopped, turning to see what his nephew was pointing at. Amy bumped into him and grunted. Cade reached down and steadied her. "Amy?"

"Are we still sharing this?" She held up the cake.

"Ah, I forgot."

She shrugged and started to step away toward the sidewalk to walk home. "We can do it another night. I understand if you're tired. Just add it to your bucket list." She grinned, but he gently held her elbow to halt her retreat.

"No, I definitely want to try it out tonight. Come on over." She allowed him to lead her toward his house, Rilan flanking her on the other side.

"What's in the box?"

"Only the best thing since sliced bread," Amy replied.

"Is it cake? Cookies?"

"Does it matter? Because you aren't getting any." She laughed as his face fell. "Kidding. You can have a bite... or two."

"Thanks." His face brightened as Cade opened the front door. He walked over to the kitchen, the open concept space inviting with their warm color schemes. Cade pointed to a stool at the kitchen bar and opened a cabinet, withdrawing two wine glasses. He then perused his cupboards and refrigerator and sighed. "Well, apparently I don't have any wine, so it looks like we will have to have the house special tonight."

Amy leaned her chin in her hands as she watched him take a gallon of milk and fill their glasses. He slid her one and she smiled. "My favorite." He grabbed a small plate and pointed to her box. She slid it to him, and he opened the lid. His eyes widened at the size of the slice.

"Whoa."

"Yeah, you have to commit to it, Cade. I hope you're prepared."

He chuckled as he lifted it onto the plate. "Want to sit outside?"

"Sure." She took their glasses as he grabbed utensils and the cake and walked to the rear sliding glass door that led to his back porch. Amy sat in one of the comfortable wooden chairs and set his wine glass of milk on the metal-framed table between them. Cade placed the cake down and flicked a light switch and a string of small lanterns dimly lit the porch.

"Hard to believe tomorrow is Monday."

"Ready for week two, Mr. Wickerson?"

"Bring it on." He toasted his glass to hers and handed her a fork. They each dug into the cake and took a bite. Cade paused as the bite hit his taste buds and Amy's smile grew even bigger.

"Rocks your world, doesn't it?"

"Wow. Seriously." Cade took another sip of his milk. "I don't know how you eat this whole thing."

"I don't. Well, not in one sitting any way. I typically get a piece and eat on it throughout the week."

"I can see why. It's super rich, but dang... it's delicious." He took another bite and she grinned. "I think this tops off a pretty great weekend."

"I'm glad." She sighed as she leaned back in her chair and folded her feet under herself.

"You dressing up as anyone this week?"

"Nope. We are recapping what they remember from their previous U.S. History classes, which for most of them was three years ago, so I will have the desks split down the middle tomorrow."

"What for?"

"Why, don't you know about the Civil War, Mr. Wickerson?" she teased.

"Interesting. You're dividing your class up North versus South."

"Yes. Though each of them will be assigned an identity when they walk in and as we go through the week, desks will move based on allegiances, deaths, peace treaties, etc. Eventually the desks are pretty much merged back to where they were last week."

"And how's that?"

"Because despite other topics we will cover, the idea is that it all helped make us the *United* States we are today. And they'll see that even though both sides experienced losses and victories at different points throughout the war, the outcome impacted the country as a whole, not just the individual sides themselves."

"Tough concept to teach when you have to work in all the other factors involved."

"Yep. But they need to know what our country went through in order to understand it now."

"That's true. It will be neat to hear what they think."

"What about you?" she asked. "What's your week look like?"

"We start Romeo and Juliet this week."

"Have to get that Shakespeare out of the way early to make way for the good stuff?"

He laughed. "Something like that."

"I have a Shakespeare wig if you want to borrow it."

Cade smirked until he saw that she was serious. "You really have one?"

"Yeah. I use it for several characters. But I have been William Shakespeare a time or two. I also have a really great ruff if you want to use it."

"What is a ruff?"

"You know, the big floosy collar that sort of ruffles out."

Laughing, Cade shook his head. "I think I'll pass, but thanks."

"Oh, come on, it would be funny."

"I think I will stick with recitations."

"So boring." She winked at him as she took a bite and then set her fork down. "I need to stop, or I will eat way too much of this tonight." She swallowed the last of her milk.

Cade set his fork down as well.

"Finished?" Amy asked and stood reaching for the plate. "I'll go give it to Rilan."

He wiped his mouth as she slid the door open and called the teen's name. Cade saw his nephew walk up and accept the plate with a pleased smile and wandered back off.

"I should probably head home since it's a school night."

Cade stood and walked her through the house toward the front door and out onto the porch. "Are you walking home?"

"Yep."

"Give me a second to find my shoes and I'll go with you."

"Don't worry about it."

"No, I want to. I don't like the idea of you walking in the dark by yourself."

"It's only a couple of blocks, Cade. I do it all the time."

"That was before you met me. Now that you have, I will walk you home when I can."

He could tell Amy wanted to smart back a sarcastic retort, but surprised him with a simple, "Thanks."

He slipped into his sneakers and told Rilan where he was going.

"Later, kid," Amy called to him, and he mouthed a goodbye around an enormous bite of chocolate cake.

"Thanks for sharing your delicious dessert with us." Cade kept pace with her as she started walking the familiar pathway to her street.

"You're welcome. Thanks for the company."

They walked in silence a moment. Cade wondered what Amy thought of his dinner with Suzanne. He was astonished she hadn't asked for more information about it, but she kept quiet as their feet scuffed against the sidewalk.

"When do you visit James again?" he asked, breaking the quiet.

"Not sure." She shrugged.

"Sounds like you had a great time with them the other night."

"I did. They're wonderful people. If I receive another dinner invite, I will most definitely go, but I want it to be on their terms. I don't want to impose on Peter's time with James every time he's in town."

"Even though James thinks you're his 'Heart's Love?'"

Amy's smile turned sweet. "Oh James, such a sweet talker."

"And great kisser," Cade teased.

Amy laughed. "That too. I can only imagine how passionate his kiss would have been fifty years ago." She fanned her face and Cade grinned as they walked up her front porch steps. She unlocked her door and turned. "Thanks for the walk, again. It's becoming a habit."

"I'm okay with that." Cade flashed a smile and she flushed. He took a step toward her, and she froze, her eyes shooting up to his. She was petite, the top of her head barely reaching him mid chest, but she tilted her head back to look up at him. He gently brushed a strand of her hair and let it trail through his fingers. Soft and silky, it slipped through and fell back to her shoulder. When he realized what he'd done, he cleared his throat and took a cautious step back. "I better head back." His voice was barely above a whisper and her calm hazel eyes held his a brief moment longer before she blinked and took a step over her threshold.

"Good night, Cade." She started to close the door and he reached a hand out, his palm preventing it from shutting. Her brows rose as his brown eyes zeroed in on her.

He wanted to kiss her. It'd been on his mind for days since she first spoke of her interaction with James. And every time he was near her, he found himself only wanting to know her more. He thought Suzanne might help take away what he thought he was feeling toward Amy, but all it did was make him wish to spend time with Amy more. But he couldn't kiss her now. He had literally been on a date with another woman earlier that night. What would that say about his character then?

"Cade?" Wary, she studied him curiously.

He shook his head and lowered his hand as he fumbled with his words. "I... um... just wanted to say thanks again... for the cake."

She leaned her head against the edge of the door and smiled. "You're welcome. See you tomorrow."

"Night, Amy." As the door shut, he kicked himself for his awkwardness. He'd only known her a few weeks, and he had to remind himself that he worked with her. Any thoughts of a relationship other than a professional one would only make their situation awkward if things did not work out. Frustrated, he jogged the rest of the way home, hoping, so as to avoid questions, that Rilan had already called it a night.

CHAPTER THIRTEEN

Amy waited patiently in her seat as Mr. Dawson, the principal, walked to the podium and rang a small bell to grab everyone's attention.

"Afternoon, everyone," he greeted as everyone found his or her seat. His warm brown gaze surveyed the room and then went back to his notepad. Amy stared at the small spot on his head where his salt and pepper hair had begun to thin and waited for him to kick off the meeting.

"I want to thank you all for staying a bit later this afternoon. I'll try to make this quick so you can all get home. It's that time of year where spirits are high for the big homecoming game next week," Mr. Dawson continued a spiel that Amy had inadvertently tuned out. "We must remember that the dress up days must still follow our dress code policy, so be sure to enforce it."

Rachel elbowed her. "What are you thinking about?"

"Nothing."

"Cade?" Rachel whispered with a smirk.

"No. I'm thinking about what costumes I want to use this year."

Knowing full well that was exactly what Amy had been thinking about, Rachel tried to hide her disappointment. She wanted her friend to think of Cade. Over the last couple of weeks, Cade had grown close with them, particularly Amy. The two had a seamless friendship that carried over to their classrooms. They teased one another and played pranks on one another. They were all the students could talk about the last few weeks as their heated prank war continued to ramp up. It was all in good fun. The screws missing from Cade's podium so that when he leaned on it, he zoomed toward the floor. Amy's potted plants mysteriously switched with the Ficus trees in the main lobby so that instead of a cute plant on her desk, a giant tree awaited her. The students loved it. And Rachel knew Amy did as well. What she didn't know was if there was something more between the two. She sensed there was, but ever since Cade's date with Suzanne, and a few other nights out with the home ec teacher, whispers of him and Amy in a budding relationship had faded.

"Now, if Suzanne could come and share with you all about fundraising for Homecoming. Suzanne?" Mr. Dawson waved her forward. Suzanne stood proudly and straightened her purple blouse before walking to the front. She slid behind the podium and cleared her throat. "As you all know, I have been asked to head the fundraising team for Homecoming week." She placed a hand over her heart as if it were a dream come true. Amy forced herself not to roll her eyes at the woman's antics and looked to Rachel for agreement. "I am looking for a team of teachers to help with this. Essentially, hosting meetings in their classrooms during free period, helping out at the concessions during the homecoming game, and encouraging students and their parents. Now, some after school hours may be required, but not too many. You have my word," she giggled. "So, any volunteers?"

Amy and Rachel exchanged a look as if silently trying to get on the same page of what they wanted to volunteer for.

"Ah, Mrs. Smith. Thank you." Suzanne wrote down on her notepad and glanced back up. "Coach Stanton, great, thank you. Anyone else?"

Amy avoided making eye contact with Suzanne and waited for others to volunteer. She shuddered at the thought of being on the same team as Suzanne in anything. "Ah, Mr. Wickerson, thank you." Amy's eyes widened slightly at the sound of Cade's name. *What was he thinking?* Did Aaron not tell him to not volunteer? Rachel leaned over to Amy and whispered. "Aaron must not have told him to wait for the sign-up sheet."

Amy shook her head.

"What about you two ladies?" Suzanne asked pointedly, her disapproving gaze at their whispering penetrating through them.

Amy shook her head, followed by Rachel.

"I see. Not wanting to volunteer…" She shook her head in dismay and shame. Amy and Rachel held their heads high. Both volunteered their time and efforts to other organizations at the school, but any chance Suzanne had at making them look bad she would take. Besides, Amy thought, she did plan to volunteer, but only after she saw the complete list of opportunities.

A couple more teachers held up their hands and Suzanne wrote their names down and finally left the podium.

Mr. Dawson eased behind the stand again. "All right, thank you, Suzanne, and those of you who volunteered. Now a volunteer for open classroom in the mornings prior to the bell so students can work on float materials?"

Amy raised her hand quickly.

"Yes, Ms. Frasier, thank you."

Rachel raised her hand too. "And Ms. Cline, perfect."
He wrote their names down and moved along with the agenda.

"I thought we were going to wait for the list?" Rachel whispered to Amy.

"I would have if he didn't announce the one thing I wanted."

Rachel smirked as she leaned back in her chair. "No volunteering. Take that Suzanne," Rachel whispered to Amy, making her chuckle.

∞

Cade watched as Amy and Rachel volunteered to be the early morning open classrooms and their constant whispering back and forth. He wondered what he might have gotten himself into volunteering for Suzanne's team. By the look Aaron shot him when he did, it must not have been good. Suzanne would have been disappointed if he hadn't, and she seemed pleased he offered to help her. He heard Mr. Dawson dismiss the group and stood.

"Oh, Mr. Wickerson," Suzanne grabbed his arm. "I wanted to invite you to Burgundy's Bar tonight. Several of us gather together to plan for the Homecoming festivities."

He'd yet to be invited to one of the Burgundy Bar nights. He knew Amy had been invited a few times by Coach Stanton, but he wasn't sure if she ever went. He didn't think so. But then again, she knew what to expect in the upcoming week. This would be his first big week of P.S. 14 tradition. Maybe it would be good for him to meet with part of the teacher team and collaborate.

"Sure, that sounds fun. What's the address?"

Suzanne's smile widened. "Oh, you know, I'm not sure. It's somewhere downtown. I can drive there, but I couldn't tell you the exact address off the top of my head. I can swing by and pick you up tonight if you like?"

For sake of ease, Cade agreed. He'd need to make sure there was food in the house. He'd yet to make it to the grocery store this week and he and Rilan both were tired of cereal. He couldn't leave his nephew at home without some sort of meal.

Not a problem. He'd just buzz by there on the way home. Rilan had hitched a ride with his buddy, Ryan, after school when he found out Cade had a staff meeting. The two teens may have already grabbed some grub. "Sure. Sounds great." She flashed a dazzling smile and told him she would pick him up at six. He wound his way out of the room and found Aaron waiting for him, twirling his car keys on his pointer finger. The man had constant energy, and as Cade grew to know Aaron better, he noticed several ticks the guy had. The car keys on the finger, the constant pencil thumping on the desk, or the incessant foot tapping whenever he sat. Aaron eyed him curiously.

"You going to Burgundy's?"

Cade nodded. "I think so. You going?"

"Yep, pretty much everyone goes. Homecoming week is a blast for the students as well as the teachers. It's really one of the few weeks out of the year we are all on the same page."

"That's good to hear." Cade ran a hand through his hair. "I wasn't quite sure what I signed up for after you shot me that look."

"Oh, you'll have your hands full with Suzanne," Aaron whispered. "Most people wait for the sign-up sheet before volunteering. But you're a newbie. I forgot to warn you."

"Maybe it won't be so bad, especially if other teachers go to Burgundy's and help plan." Cade looked to Aaron for confirmation, and he raised one shoulder in a brief 'I don't know' gesture.

"Well, see you later, then." Aaron gave a quick pat on Cade's back and jogged to his truck.

Cade watched Amy climb into her car and wondered if she would be at Burgundy's later. As he watched her back out of the parking lot, she cast him a friendly salute and smile. He hoped she'd be there.

∞

Amy pulled into Aaron's driveway and waved as she spotted Rilan and Ryan tossing a football in Cade's front yard. "Hey, you two!" She waved them over. "I need some extra hands." She popped her trunk, and they hustled over.

"What are those?" Rilan asked, looking at the giant plastic tubs in her backseat.

"They're my costume arsenal." She smiled as she moved out of the way for each of them to lift the heavy tubs. She jogged to unlock Aaron's door and pointed to the middle of the living room. "You can just put them there. Thanks."

The boys set the tubs down and Rilan rested his hands on his hips, a stance that mirrored Cade when he stood up front in his classroom. She grinned. "What?" he asked curiously.

"You look like your uncle when you do that." She pointed at his hands and Rilan dropped them on an eye roll. "Are these the only tubs in your car?"

"No, I have one more in the trunk and a couple of bags."

"Gosh, Ms. Frazzle, what do you do with all these costumes? Are they all your history people?"

"Most are, but some are just for fun. From homecoming weeks past. You guys been thinking about who you want to ask to the dance?" Both boys flushed at her question. "I take that as a yes."

"Well, I want to take Taylor Parsons," Ryan stated proudly. "Pretty sure she'll say yes. She's been flirting with me for like two weeks."

Amy laughed at his confidence. "Well, that is a good sign. What about you, kid?"

Rilan shrugged. "Not sure. I don't exactly have girls lining up like Ryan does."

"Yeah right." Ryan shoved Rilan and just shook his head.

A horn honked, and Cade's truck pulled into the driveway next to them. He hopped out with a friendly smile. "What's going on, guys?"

Rilan pointed at Amy. "Helping our chameleon with all her alter egos."

Amy laughed and moved out of the way so he could grab the remaining tub. Ryan grabbed the two paper bags and both boys took them inside. "Costumes," Amy explained. "Rachel and Aaron always raid my collection for homecoming week. You're welcome to dig through as well, if you need any."

He opened his mouth to respond, but another car horn honked and pulled to the curb. Suzanne. He glanced at his watch. "Wow, I thought I'd have more time."

Rilan and Ryan exited Aaron's house and Amy caught Rilan's disapproving glance at Suzanne's car. "You going out tonight? Again?" he asked.

"Um, yeah." Cade shifted on his feet a bit. "I didn't realize it was already six. Several teachers are getting together to plan for homecoming week."

"You going?" Rilan asked Amy.

She shook her head.

"You're not?" Cade asked, surprised.

"No. I think Rachel and Aaron are though."

"Why aren't you going?" Cade asked.

Amy shrugged. "Because I don't want to." She offered a small smile.

"But I thought pretty much everyone goes."

"They do."

"But not you." His tone hardened a bit, and she tilted her head to gauge why he seemed to be getting upset.

"Not always, no. I am going to be sorting through what I just unloaded in Aaron's house."

"You should come." Cade pointed to Suzanne's car. "You can ride with us."

The thought made Amy cringe, but she just shook her head. "No thanks. You guys have fun. I'll hear what everyone comes up with later."

"So, no food?" Rilan asked Cade.

"Sorry, I planned to go to the store before heading over there. I thought she was picking me up a bit later."

Rilan nodded, but disappointment shadowed his usually smiling face.

"I'll feed you," Amy offered. "You too, Ryan, if you're sticking around for a bit." She looked to Cade. "I don't mind."

Regret washed over Cade's face, but he saw the hope in his nephew's face at not having to suffer through cereal for the third night in a row. "If you want," he told Rilan.

Rilan fist bumped Amy in thanks and nodded. Ryan shook his head. "I can't. I have to take my sister to ballet practice tonight since my mom's out of town."

"Well, thanks for helping with the tubs, Ryan," Amy said.

He nodded and slapped Rilan on the back as he walked toward his beat-up car. "See ya tomorrow, Wickerson," he called to Rilan as he backed out of the driveway.

"Rilan can help me go through costumes," Amy added. "So, his meal is not charity, he has to work for it." She grinned as Rilan made a face.

"Do I have to try any on?"

"Only if you want to."

"Deal."

"Well, when you're done eating, I want you to make sure all your homework is done before I get home. And lights out by ten. You have a test tomorrow," Cade continued.

"Uncle Cade, dude, chill. I'll be fine. I've stayed by myself quite a bit lately. I know the drill." Amy could see that statement made Cade feel bad in an instant.

Suzanne took a half step out of her car. "Cade!" she called, with a wave for him to hurry.

Cade reached for his wallet.

"Don't even think about it," Amy told him. "Go. I got this. We'll be fine."

"Alright," Cade slid his wallet back into his back pocket. "Thanks. And I promise I will go to the grocery store tomorrow," he told Rilan as he walked toward an awaiting Suzanne.

They watched as Cade hopped into her car and Suzanne flashed a forced smile at Amy as she pulled away from the curb. "I won't hold my breath," Rilan muttered.

Amy gave him a sympathetic smile. "Come on, let's lock up Aaron's house and go get some grub. I have some great cereal, if you're interested."

Rilan audibly groaned, making her laugh.

"Kidding. What are you in the mood for?"

"Anything."

"How about I call something in at Romero's and have it delivered, then we don't have to go anywhere."

"Romero's? That Italian place?"

"Yep."

"That sounds amazing. But isn't it kind of expensive?"

Amy shrugged. "It's worth it. I eat there at least once a week."

"I have yet to eat there."

"What?" Shocked, Amy held a hand to her chest. "Then scratch the whole staying at home. We're going. Give me a sec." She darted toward Aaron's house and locked the door and then motioned for Rilan to get in her car. He obeyed with a hopeful smile on his face. "Prepare yourself, Rilan Wickerson, because your world is about to change."

He laughed as she headed down the street.

CHAPTER FOURTEEN

"*You could have told* me Amy wasn't coming," Cade cornered Aaron at his first opportunity. Taken aback, Aaron took a sip of his beer. "I didn't realize it mattered."

"Well, she is across the hall from me. Thought we could plan some stuff together." His reasoning fell flat, and Aaron grinned behind his bottle.

"Right. Well, I'm sure you and Ames can pow-wow another night, if it means that much to you."

Cade growled in frustration at his own folly and embarrassment. Aaron slapped him on the shoulder. "So, what all does Suzanne have you doing for homecoming week?"

"Everything she's doing," Cade replied and Aaron only laughed harder.

"Not really funny at this point. I didn't know what all I was signing up for."

"For homecoming? Or with Suzanne in general?"

"Both," Cade admitted. "I also feel like a complete jerk right now because Amy is feeding my nephew dinner because I made plans to go out tonight."

"Did she offer?" Aaron asked.

"Yes."

"Then don't feel bad. She wouldn't have offered if she didn't mean it. Just relax, man."

Cade jumped as Suzanne walked up and draped an arm over his shoulders. "There you are." She beamed at Aaron. "I signed us up for helping with the football team's float."

"I thought we were already helping with the Homecoming Court float?"

"Well, we were, but Rachel and Amy are apparently doing that one," Suzanne explained.

"And we can't just help them?"

"I'm trying to spread out the work," Suzanne continued smoothly, though her reasoning sounded rehearsed. "And have you signed up to work on a float, Aaron?" she asked.

"Helping Rachel and Ames. Also, Eric asked me to help with the girls' basketball float."

"Ah. Good."

Cade shrugged her arm off his shoulders. "Excuse me." He walked away in a huff and Suzanne eyed Aaron warily. "What's wrong with him tonight? Why is he upset?"

Aaron shrugged. "Not sure. I know he was pretty bummed Amy didn't come tonight."

Suzanne rolled her eyes. "He sees her *all* day."

"They're friends, Suzanne," Aaron pointed out.

"Right. Of course. Well, I'm going to go mingle." She walked away stiffly, and Aaron chuckled to himself.

"You upsetting Suzanne?" Rachel asked as she walked forward.

"Nope. Cade is."

"Say wha—???" Rachel's eyes sparkled.

"Apparently, he's upset Amy didn't come, and Suzanne's upset because *he's* upset Amy didn't come." Aaron wriggled his fingers in the air as if counting to make sure he got all the right words in the right places. "The teacher loop is abuzz."

Rachel laughed. "Ay yi yi. When are they all going to get a clue?"

"For real." He pointed his beer toward Cade standing in a corner, his cell phone pressed against his ear.

"Come on, Amy, pick up," Cade muttered as he listened to the phone ring on the other side.

"Hey," she greeted.

"Amy, hey, it's Cade."

"I know." He could hear her smile into the phone and then a muffled laugh as she responded to someone else in the background. "What's up?"

"I was just... checking in."

"Cade, it's been an hour."

He looked at his watch. "Right. Well..."

"Here." She handed the phone to Rilan.

"Hey, Uncle Cade," Rilan's voice flooded over the line.

"Hey, how are things? You get your homework done?"

"Yep. Actually, I didn't have homework tonight, so I don't have any to work on."

"And you've eaten?"

"Doing that now. Amy brought me to Romero's. Uncle Cade," His voice grew serious. "This place is awesome."

Cade smiled into the phone. "I'm glad you like it. Sounds like you're feasting, while I'm having to eat bar nuts."

"You could always join us," Rilan invited. "We haven't gotten our food yet, but Amy ordered some sort of appetizer that is pretty much just a ball of cheese. It's delicious."

"Sounds like it. I might take you up on it. Need to see what all I have to do here."

"Oh wait, you can't leave early, can you? Because you rode with Ms. Meters."

"Right..." Cade contemplated his dilemma and sighed.

"What's wrong, Uncle Cade, sounds like you aren't having fun."

"It's fine. Hey, put Amy back on, will ya?"

"Sure thing. Later." He heard the transfer of hands.

"Yes?" Amy asked in a cheery voice. "Did he just make you jealous? Talking about cheese?"

Cade grinned. "Actually, he did. Think you'll be there for a while?"

"Probably. It's pretty busy tonight and service is a bit slow."

"I'm coming."

"Cade, whoa, what? Why? Are you already finished at Burgundy's?"

"No, but I need some air, and Romero's with you sounds way more fun than this place is."

"Alright. Need a ride?"

"I'll find one."

"See you in a bit. I'll have some chocolate cake waiting for you."

"You're an angel." He heard her laugh as she hung up. He then searched his phone apps to find the car service he wanted and scheduled a pick-up outside the bar.

"There you are? Everything fine at home?" Suzanne asked, gently resting a hand on his arm.

Cade shoved his phone in his pocket. "Yes, but I'm going to head out."

"Why? Everyone's finally wrapping up with their planning sessions and now it will just be fun."

"Yeah, this isn't really my scene, Suzanne."

"So? It's not exactly everyone's scene, but we are all here to have fun together. To mingle outside of the hallways. Become friends. Or more." She slid her hand to his and squeezed.

He immediately dropped it. "Yeah, I'm not interested in more. I'm sorry, but I just... my priorities weren't where they should have been tonight."

"You mean, Amy? You're leaving to go see Amy, aren't you?"

"Yes and no. I am going to see her, but I meant my nephew. Look, it's complicated, but he should be my priority right now, and I've sort of dropped the ball the last few weeks."

"I see." Though her tone clearly told him she didn't. Her eyes narrowed. "Well, see you tomorrow." She turned and her heels clicked furiously after her.

He tried to gauge his feelings as he watched her retreating back. He saw a pair of headlights outside the window, and he knew his ride had arrived and all he felt was relief.

∞

Amy held her stomach as she laughed, and Rilan continued sharing some of his and Cade's exploits over the course of the last few years. Cade's bloopers as a new parent had Amy grinning from ear to ear as Rilan spoke of his uncle in a teasing manner, but also with an enormous amount of love. The kid also dug into his meal as if he hadn't eaten in weeks, which she also knew was not the truth, but she could not imagine feeding a teenage boy on a daily basis. His appetite was three times as big as hers and she was not a light eater. Suddenly Rilan interrupted his own story. "Hey, Uncle Cade." He smiled in greeting as Cade slid into the booth next to Amy.

"Hey guys." He immediately reached for Rilan's water and took a long sip.

Timothy walked up and Amy gave him a small signal. "I ordered your food about five minutes ago. I hope you like lasagna."

He turned to her and smiled. "Yes. Thanks."

"Rilan was just telling me about some of your adventures together."

Cade's face flushed. "Not about the apartment in Shreveport?" he asked.

"Oh yeah." Rilan nodded as Amy laughed.

Cade poked her in the side as he chuckled along. "Hey now, it was not funny."

"I'm sure it wasn't at the time. So how was Burgundy's?"

Sighing, Cade leaned back in the booth and relaxed, the first time he had that evening. He draped his arm over the back of the seat. "It was okay."

"You didn't last very long," Rilan pointed out.

"He was afraid he was missing out on too much fun." Amy teased. "And Romero's." Rilan agreed and Cade's face remained serious. Amy's smile slightly faltered. "Everything okay?" she asked.

"I just... I think I made Suzanne upset, but I just couldn't stay there." His eyes washed over her face and settled briefly on her lips before diverting to the plate Timothy slid in front of him.

Rilan studied his uncle's face, the teen's expression changing from concern to amusement. "I'm glad you aren't pursuing Ms. Meters. She doesn't like me."

"What?" Cade looked up in surprise. "Why do you say that?"

"I can tell." Rilan shrugged off the rejection of a teacher he didn't care for or plan to take classes from and pointed at Amy. "But Amy's cool. She feeds me."

"How easily you're swayed." Amy laughed as she nudged him the rest of her pasta and he eagerly dove into it with his fork.

"See." Rilan beamed with a full mouth and Cade just shook his head.

Amy's phone buzzed and she saw a text flash across the screen. "Oh, sorry. I have to take this..." Her voice trailed off as she read the short message from Lucille, James's caretaker. "It's about James."

"Everything okay?" Cade asked, knowing how much the older gentleman had come to mean to Amy over the last several weeks.

"Your old boyfriend?" Rilan asked. "He okay?"

A tender smile washed over her face at their mutual concern for the man and she nodded. "She said he was asking when I'd be dropping by again to visit. When he's coherent, or in the present, he sometimes asks the same question over and over again due to his memory lapses in between. Apparently, he's asked her seven times today when I am coming to play cards again."

"And when do you plan on going?" Cade asked.

"Tomorrow after school, actually. I've organized the Student Council into volunteer hours at the assisted living home, so I will be there with about ten kiddos."

"Did you sign up?" He asked Rilan.

"No sir. I don't know much about it."

"Meaning you aren't sure if it's cool or not?" Cade rolled his eyes as Rilan shrugged. "Guess what, Ms. Frasier, you have a new Student Council member." Cade waved his hand toward his nephew and Rilan did not dispute the assignment.

"It's fun, I promise," Amy assured him.

"And I'll go too." Cade took a bite of his lasagna and leaned back against the booth seat on a long sigh. "That's ridiculously good."

Amy grinned up at him. "Chocolate cake, nachos, lasagna... I promise to introduce you to something healthy soon."

"I'm not complaining." Cade took another bite.

"Me either. Beats cereal." Rilan flinched after his comment, not wanting to upset Cade or make him feel bad.

"Fair dig." Cade held a hand to his chest. "And I'm sorry. I've been distracted lately and haven't put you first. But that changes tonight. My priority is you and making sure you like it here and are taken care of."

"I'm fine, Uncle Cade."

"No, you're not. You shouldn't have to eat bowls of cereal for breakfast and supper three days in a row. I'm ashamed to even say that aloud."

Amy patted his arm. "You've been busy too. Don't beat yourself up. Both of you are welcome to eat at my place any time. I warn you, though, I'm not the most creative cook in the world."

"That'd be fun." Rilan perked up at spending more time with her and Amy found Cade's serious gaze settled on her face once again. She couldn't tell what was going through his head, but without warning, Cade leaned toward her and kissed her cheek, lingering a moment before turning back to his plate.

Surprised, Amy's eyes widened before she felt the slight flutters in her belly and the pleasing tingle in her toes. "W-what was that for?"

Rilan, wide-eyed and silent, watched and waited with his fork poised mid-bite to see how his uncle responded.

"Just a thank you, Amy. Thank you." Cade finished his lasagna in silence as Rilan quizzed her about Student Council and who all would be part of the group tomorrow at the retirement home. She answered all his questions, sensing his nerves at trying something new, but her thoughts lingered upon her response to Cade's feather-like kiss on her cheek. She didn't see him pay the check, but when all were finished with their meal, he motioned her toward the doorway with a simple, "I took care of it."

"Guess he's bumming a meal *and* a ride off of us tonight." Rilan tossed a thumb over his shoulder toward Cade as he held the door for another departing couple and she and Rilan walked towards her car.

"Such a moocher," Amy teased and had Rilan laughing. "But a nice one."

Rilan nudged her elbow, breaking her trance on Cade standing at the door and she blinked in surprise. The smirk on Rilan's face had her blushing, but she ignored it as she slid into the driver's seat of her car and started the engine. Cade pointed for Rilan to move to the backseat, the teen shaking his head in denial. "I believe you're the third wheel in this event, Uncle Cade, so I've got dibs."

Laughing, Amy waited while Cade folded his long legs into the back seat on a grunt, his knees bumping the back of Rilan's seat with more force than necessary and the teen dramatically shifting against the cushion to push back.

"Alright, you two." Amy giggled as she drove to Cade's house and both Wickersons bantered back and forth about their day, the evening, and scheduling for the next few days. She enjoyed hearing them chat. Cade's love for his nephew was obvious and Rilan's respect for Cade evident with his acquiescence to his uncle's final say. Their life together hadn't been easy, she was sure of that, but over the years a priceless bond had formed between the two, and she could tell they cherished one another. She pulled to a stop behind Cade's truck in his driveway and Rilan hopped out quickly. Cade replaced him in the front seat and shut the door, his nephew turning around to see why his uncle hadn't followed. Cade waved him onward to the house and waited until he was inside before turning to Amy.

"Thank you, again, for a great evening and for spending time with Rilan. I appreciate it."

"No problem. He's a great kid, Cade. You've done well." She patted his hand, and he held it a moment, covering it with his other one. Her heart started its rhythmic jump. Cade sat quietly, his gaze wandering from their hands to out the window, his jaw clenched. She squeezed his hand and brought his gaze back to hers and a sad smile washed over his face.

"Thanks for saying that." His voice was gruff, and he inhaled a deep breath and released her hand. "I'll let you get home."

"I meant what I said about eating together. Anytime."

"I like the idea." Cade exited with a smile and leaned in once more to look at her. "And I'm glad our paths have crossed, Amy. I think you're one of the reasons this year is already shaping up to be a good one."

"It's only been a few weeks. I think you're giving me too much credit. And if I keep feeding you such unhealthy food, you and your waistline may end up disliking me."

"I can't even fathom such a thing," he complimented. "See you tomorrow at school."

He started to close the door. "Wait!" Amy called, and he ducked his head back in the door frame. "Carpool?"

"Would love to. I'll pick you up." He closed the door, and she watched as her headlights illuminated his long and lean figure while he walked across the yard to his front door. He tossed one more friendly wave before disappearing inside. Amy released a heavy breath and shifted into reverse. "Tread carefully, Amy," she warned herself. "Tread carefully."

CHAPTER FIFTEEN

"*That's four tens added* to the three that are already there, which means I just made another canasta." Amy tucked her cards into a neat pile and discarded a queen of hearts. "Your turn."

Rilan ran a hand over his chin and James leaned over and peeked at his cards. "You want to take that." He pointed to the discarded queen. "Trust me, young man, a pretty lady doesn't come around often, especially when you have two in your hand already." Rilan took the advice and laid his two queens on the table and fished in the discard pile for the set number of cards he needed in order to draw from the stack. James nodded in approval. "He's learning."

Amy smiled with a friendly nod. "He'll be beating us soon."

"I doubt that. You've got the mind and the luck for this game, Amy dear."

Cade walked up and sat in the empty chair next to Amy. "Who's winning?"

"Hard to say." James pointed to Rilan as the teen laid stack after stack of card groupings onto the table, unloading his hand and already moving into his second hand of cards that needed to be played before he could end the round.

Cade beamed proudly. "Well, all the other students seem to have found friends. We have a chess match going, checkers, scrabble, and dominoes."

"And what about you, young man?" James asked, looking to Cade with a knowing smile as Cade lingered near Amy's side. "What's your game of choice?"

"Looks like I need to learn Canasta if my nephew plans to practice." He scooted his chair closer to Amy and watched as she shifted her cards in her hands, pointing to several he assumed were good picks.

"I had a feeling you'd choose cards." James chuckled as Rilan discarded and waved for him to start his turn. His two cards stuck together, the worn deck having seen better days, as decades of use wore their edges. James licked his thumb and attempted to draw again, this time successfully pulling two cards.

"How long have you played this game?" Rilan asked.

James, his fingers shifting and moving cards around in his hand, briefly glanced at him over the top of his glasses. "Since my honeymoon."

"Your honeymoon?" Amy asked. "And how long ago was that?"

"Oh, let's see now—" James tallied his fingers in the air, "Fifty-eight years ago, on the balcony of a bed and breakfast in Manuel Antonio, Costa Rica to be exact."

Cade's brows rose. "Wow. Now that sounds like an adventure."

"Oh, it was." James smiled. "My Becca and I explored the entire country for our honeymoon. And she taught me how to play Canasta in the evenings while we enjoyed sunset after sunset."

"Sounds magical." Amy took her turn and attempted to show and explain her reasonings to Cade so he could learn to play.

"Yes, my Becca was one of a kind," James continued, nodding toward Amy. "Much like this one."

"You loved her very much," Amy stated, giving James even more encouragement to continue sharing his story. Cade wanted to know more about his eccentric wife as well.

"Amy mentioned Becca was in the circus. Can you tell us more about that?" Cade asked.

"The circus?" Rilan sat up straighter in his seat. "No way."

James laughed. "She was. Most of our early years of marriage were traveling with the big top. I'd travel around selling books, magazines, newspapers, and even men's shaving kits and she'd send me a postcard from wherever she was located. I'd meet her there, spend a week or so with her at the circus and then I'd go back to work, and she'd move to the next city. We travelled all over the country. Didn't have our first home until our fifth wedding anniversary."

"What was her act in the circus?" Rilan asked. "Trapeze? Fortune Teller?"

"Oh, no. My Becca was a magician." James pointed to the deck of cards. "And these were some of the cards she used in some of her acts."

"That's awesome." Rilan smiled at Amy and Cade before turning his attention back to James.

"She was." James smiled. "It was rare having a female magician in those days, which only made her act even better. She was eye-catching, breathtaking, and phenomenal. Yes, all those things." James watched Rilan make his next move and nodded in approval as he reached for the deck in front of him to take his turn. "She was so beautiful there in the ring. She always wore different outfits and costumes, but her face was always radiant. I loved her very much. My heart will always love her."

"And that's why she is your heart's love," Amy added. "The nickname you gave her."

"Yes. Yes, she is..." His voice wavered and his hand hesitated over the discard pile. "Did I draw?"

"Yes." Rilan pointed out. "You were about to discard."

James looked up at Rilan, his eyes narrowed. "Who are you?"

Cade studied his nephew to see how he'd react to the older man's confusion.

"I'm the teenage hooligan who's about to whoop you in cards."

James hooted in laughter, his eyes turning to Cade and Amy. When they landed on Amy, he beamed. "I don't know where you found this one, Becca love, but he sure makes me laugh. Is he new?"

Cade gently squeezed Amy's knee, knowing it made her a bit sad when James would confuse her for Becca. Her hand rested upon his as she laid her deck of cards down on the table. "He is. His name is Rilan. And this is his first time to play cards with you."

"What's the score?" James asked.

Amy read him the numbers.

"I guess I'm a good teacher then." James looked to Cade and sized him up, his eyes flickering to their hands beneath the table. "Amy?" James's voice was uncertain. "I-I'm sorry, I think I forgot where we were at."

Brief and momentarily, James was back in the present again, though he still didn't recognize Rilan or Cade. He extended his hand to Cade. "You've got yourself a good one here." He pointed at Amy. "Reminds me of my Becca. Beautiful and smart. Best grab her up while you can. I noticed the lunch man makin' eyes at her today."

Amy laughed. "I don't know if Steven was making eyes at me. I think he was just surprised at how much mac and cheese I piled on my plate."

"You two suit one another." James leaned back in his chair and studied them, Amy's cheeks flushing as she picked up her cards and tried to busy her hands. Cade rubbed an embarrassed hand over the back of his neck and avoided Rilan's pleased expression. "Best not wait long, boy," James continued. "Women like Amy pull on the heart. If she hasn't yours yet, she will on another soon enough. Trust me. You don't wait. You just jump." He handed his cards to Rilan. "I'm done. I win."

Rilan smothered a laugh at the man's declaration. "But I beat you by over a thousand points."

"I let you beat me, therefore, I'm actually better." James patted Rilan gently on the shoulder as he waved to Lucille. "I enjoyed our time together." He shook Rilan's hand and then Cade's. "And Amy girl, you make him treat you to a nice dinner, alright? You deserve it."

"I'll do my best, James."

"And tell Peter I'm okay."

"I will."

He waved as Lucille rolled his wheelchair away. Amy gently stacked all the cards into a deck and put them in a small plastic box on the table. "I'll give these to Lucille when she comes back so he has them. Thanks for playing. He was extremely lucid today, which was wonderful."

"I like him." Rilan nodded at one of the teenage girls, a member of Student Council, that walked by with an elderly lady talking to her about the ins and outs of quilting. The girl blushed at Rilan's acknowledgment.

"I see you've gotten someone's attention." Amy wriggled her eyebrows at him, and Cade noticed the light pink tint to Rilan's neck.

"She's nice. Don't know her too well."

"Homecoming is coming up," Amy reminded him. "Plan on asking anyone to the big game and dance?"

Rilan shrugged. "I wasn't planning on it, but it seems everyone goes to the dance and it's a big deal. I just don't know who I'd ask or who would say yes."

"You still have a few weeks," Cade assured him. "No rush."

"You heard the old man," Rilan motioned over his shoulder. "You don't wait around for the good ones, Uncle Cade. You just have to jump."

"Yes, well, love is a bit different than a date for a high school dance."

"Not really." Rilan leaned back in the chair, its two back legs creaking under his weight. Amy tugged him back to all four legs. "Either way, you have to risk rejection, which completely sucks."

"But if you don't ask her, you'll never know." Amy pointed to the girl across the room.

"Can you two not talk to me about this right now?" Rilan, embarrassed, stood to his feet. "Not sure how I feel about you double teaming me."

Amy grinned as Cade laughed. "Fair enough. Go. Find another resident to meet." He waved him away and Amy turned to him with an amused smirk on her lips.

"Speaking of homecoming, float work begins tomorrow after school. You ready?"

"Considering Suzanne signed me up to help with about fifty of them, no, I'm not."

Laughing, Amy shook her head in pity. "Oh, Wickerson, you're such a newbie."

"Yes, well, some teachers, who shall remain nameless," He coughed hers, Rachel's, and Aaron's names in his hand before continuing. "Did not tell me that you don't volunteer up front. Instead, they let me make a rookie mistake. Some friends they are, right?"

She playfully punched his shoulder. "I hear they're quite awesome."

"One of them definitely is." Cade leaned toward her, his hand reaching for hers under the table once more. Her eyes danced and she didn't tug her hand away until two students walked their direction.

Amy glanced at her watch. "It's time to gather them up and head out. Mind?"

"Not at all." Cade stood, gently resting his hand at the small of her back as he called for the students to say their farewells and head to the minibus they'd brought to the center. Rilan, his steps slowing to let the cute girl catch up, gave Amy a shy smile as he opened the door for his new friend.

"And I guess he's decided to jump," Cade whispered.

"Good for him." Amy grinned up at him and Cade couldn't help but be drawn to her sweet pleasure at his nephew's growing confidence. "You okay?" She tapped his cheek in a light pat to break his trance on her face and he forced a smile.

"Fine. Yes," he bumbled. "Let's get them back to the school." He waved for her to walk ahead of him out the door, students waiting in line to load up on the bus.

"You alright, Uncle Cade?" Rilan whispered, nodding toward Amy's back as she stood in the center aisle of the bus talking with two girls about their experience at the retirement home. She laughed, turning to look back at the Wickersons, both giving her a thumbs up.

"Why wouldn't I be alright?" Cade asked.

"I can just tell something's got you thinking." Rilan nodded his head toward Amy. "You thinking about what Mr. James said?"

Cade shook his head and motioned to the driver's seat of the bus. "I need to get us moving."

"I want us to talk about it, Uncle Cade. Really."

Cade paused a minute, glancing into the concerned eyes of his brother, only instead of his brother, it was Rilan. A short, but sharp twinge hit his heart as if the grief of losing his brother threatened to spill out. Thankful for the resemblance between

Rilan and his dad, Cade nodded, too choked up to respond. Rilan patted his shoulder. "I'm totally team Amy, by the way, in case you needed any further assurance of that," Rilan whispered with a smirk as he slid into a seat next to the cute girl he'd escorted earlier.

Cade looked in the rearview mirror and Amy gave him a thumbs up that all students were accounted for; and she walked up the aisle to sit in the seat adjacent to the driver's seat. "Ready when you are, Mr. Wickerson." She smiled, the sparkle in her eyes holding him transfixed a moment before he snapped out of it and shifted the bus into gear and headed back to the school.

∞

The gym was crowded with students and teachers. Shimmering ribbons, streamers, papier-mâché, and any craft supply Amy could think of crowded around her as she and Rachel sat on the floor working on hot gluing large rose petals, made from tissue paper, together for the Homecoming Court float. Rachel leaned over and grabbed another piece of red tissue paper and began twisting and folding it and then handed it to Amy. She applied a generous amount of hot glue and pieced it together with the others and then held up the oversized fluffy flower. "Well?"

"Works for me." Rachel sprayed the flower with aerosol hairspray and then tossed a handful of glitter at it. "Tada."

Glitter sprinkled everywhere, including all over Amy. "Gee, thanks." Laughing, Amy swatted away as much as she could from her lap and stood to walk the flower over to the Student Council president, Bethany, who was in charge of their float design.

"Thanks Ms. Frasier."

"How many more do we need?" Amy asked.

Bethany glanced down at her clipboard. "Twenty-five more."

"Twenty-five?" Amy asked, baffled by the amount of time that went into the one single rose. "Alright, I better get after it then." She walked back over to Rachel and sat on the gym floor, crossing her legs beneath her as she reached for more red tissue paper. "We better chop-chop, Rachel. We have twenty-five of these suckers left."

"*Twenty-five?*" Rachel's eyes widened and she looked up at the trailer that was to be their float base. "Is this the Rose Parade or something?"

Amy stifled a laugh as she spotted Cade carrying a ladder across the gym toward one of the floats Suzanne had him appointed to. He rested it against the double-decker trailer and climbed up to intercept a garland from Suzanne out of one of the upper windows. Rachel snapped in front of her face. "If you stare any harder, people are going to think you've got eyes for him."

"I was just trying to figure out their design over there. What is that? Juliet's tower?"

"Yep," Rachel confirmed.

"What organization is riding in that? What does it have to do with anything?"

"You realize there is a literature club, right?"

"Oh, right... interesting. Why isn't there a history club?"

Rachel cackled. "You think kids want to be in a history club?"

"There's math clubs," Amy pointed out. "And obviously literature clubs. Science clubs. Why not history? It's cooler than all the others."

"Says you. *I* get to blow things up in the name of science. Now *that's* cool." Rachel smirked as Amy gave her that point.

"But seriously, Romeo and Juliet?" Amy rolled her eyes. "So many great books they could have chosen."

"They went with something sweet because they are also promoting the homecoming dance for after the game," Rachel explained. "And the theme is Shakespearean Nights."

"They do realize that Romeo and Juliet kill themselves, right? Or is that part simply glossed over these days?"

"Ask the English teacher." Rachel pointed to Cade. "I hear you have a pretty good rapport with him."

Amy went back to gluing petals and ignored Rachel's comment.

"What happened here? Did a fairy explode?" Rilan sat across from Amy and Rachel and picked up some of the red tissue paper and watched Rachel's movements as she shaped a petal. He did the same.

"Hey, kid. You're just who I needed to see. What are you doing here?"

"Uncle Cade forced me."

"Nice." Amy grinned. "And have you been suffering?" she eyed a group of cheerleaders eying him from across the room and whispering with giddy smiles on their faces.

He blushed and continued working. "You could say that."

"Did you ask Taylor to the dance?"

He shook his head. "No."

"Why not? I thought you were." Amy accepted the petal he handed her way and glued it onto her work in progress.

"She got asked by someone else."

"And she said yes?"

"Apparently."

"Lame." Amy, disappointed for him, held up their completed rose. "Well?"

His forehead crinkled and he shrugged. "Looks good to me. What's it supposed to be?"

"A rose!" Amy palmed her forehead. "Seriously? What did you think it was supposed to be?"

"I don't know... a big red blob." He grinned as she tossed it aside and pointed to the stack of tissue paper. "I have to make tons of these things, and they keep getting worse and worse. Plus, Rachel keeps showering me with glitter and hairspray and my legs are cramping from sitting like this for so long."

"Man, you sure are whining." She tossed a palmful of glitter at him and he balked at the bright and shimmering spot in the middle of his chest. "That was uncalled for."

Laughing, Amy stood to her feet. "Why don't you work on these for a bit. I'll find you some help."

"If it gets me out of Juliet's tower, then no problem." He grabbed the glue gun and set to work as Amy walked over to the group of cheerleaders and asked the one she felt was the sweetest of the bunch to help Rilan with the roses. Carrie Smithson walked up, and Rilan flushed when Amy introduced them. The girl sat and watched him a moment, asking a few questions before she hopped right to the task. In less than a handful of minutes, the two teens were chatting and smiling at one another. She assumed she'd done well there at least.

A scream pierced the air and Amy spun to see Suzanne, who had been sitting on the edge of the tower window pinning faux vines along its wall, falling from said window. She ran toward the float just as Cade did and they both caught Suzanne on her way to the ground. The three of them crashed against the gym floor and Amy felt a snap of pain shoot up her left arm at the impact. Suzanne's head popped up in surprise, her eyes narrowing at Amy and then softening at Cade as he rushed to his feet and helped her up. Amy stayed on the ground, tucking her left arm to her middle as Suzanne clung to Cade's shirt and sought comfort. Cade's gaze flashed down at her. "You alright there, Amy?" Amy flashed him a thumbs up and he gave a relieved nod as he escorted Suzanne to a chair by the snack table and tended to her.

Aaron and Rachel ran toward her as she pushed her way up off the floor with one hand. "You okay, Ames?"

She grimaced. "I think I broke my wrist." Aaron gently rested the sore arm in his palm and ran his fingers up and down the bone structure. Amy hissed.

"Looks like it."

"I'm going to go to the clinic and get it seen about." She walked over to her pile of flowers, Rilan immediately hopping to his feet.

"Amy," He hugged her. "I'll get Uncle Cade. We can take you to the doctor."

She gently cupped his face. "No, I'm fine. I can go by myself. Besides, he's a bit preoccupied. I'll just go and get an x-ray and then see you all at Aaron's later. You have fun." She tilted her head toward Carrie and gave him a reassuring smile when his young face still held worry. She patted his arm as she scooped up her purse and awkwardly draped it over her body to avoid moving her left arm.

"Message us and let us know what the doctor says." Aaron walked her to her car and opened the door for her.

"Will do. Let me know if Suzanne is okay."

Aaron bit back a rude remark and just gave a curt nod. "I will. See you later. My place. I'll have supper for all of us."

"That's a deal. See ya later." She hopped inside her car and headed to the small emergency clinic down the street. Hopefully, she would be in and out and home by the time everyone was finished at the gym. Thankful she no longer had to glue roses together, but nervous about her arm, Amy hoped the injury wouldn't be too serious. She turned into the clinic and parked, quickly making her way inside. She'd soon find out.

CHAPTER SIXTEEN

Cade paced the floor of Aaron's living room waiting for Amy to arrive. Though Suzanne had thanked him for catching her fall, the brunt of her weight had fallen to Amy. He had just lent a small help in the matter. He'd hoped to absorb more of the momentum, but he hadn't gotten there as fast as Amy. He didn't realize she'd hurt herself in the process. She just quietly exited while his attention had been on Suzanne. Rilan was furious with him for ignoring Amy. He couldn't quite convince his nephew that he hadn't meant to, but everyone was on edge about the incident because Amy hadn't come home yet from the clinic. Headlights bounced through the glass window, and Cade was out the door and halfway across the lawn when everyone else caught up.

Amy opened her car door and gasped when it slung back faster than she'd moved it. She relaxed when she saw Cade. "Hey." She eased out of the car, her left arm in a splint and sling. His heart sank.

Aaron whistled. "Nice hardware you have there."

Amy's weary smile spoke volumes as Rachel offered a comforting hug. "I've got you a cold pinot grigio in the fridge. We have risotto and steamed veggies, pork chops, and buttery bread on the stove, and I brought over some of your clothes and they're in the guestroom."

"Wow, you've thought of everything." Amy sighed as she stepped inside the house. Rilan sat at the bar waiting and immediately hopped to his feet. "Hey, kid. Did you finish my flowers for me?"

Yes ma'am." He stood awkwardly staring at her, his eyes flashing to her injury and then back up to her face. "You okay?"

"I'll live." Amy smiled and accepted the delicate and slightly awkward hug he gave her. Her eyes found Cade. "And how did you fare, Wickerson? All intact?"

"I'm fine." He gently touched the sling and shook his head. "Why did you run over there?"

"I was closest. I thought I would just sort of catch her and ease her to the ground. But she didn't exactly fall to land, she fell to be caught… and that wasn't quite the best idea. So instead of helping someone catch themselves, I was a landing pad. Not my finest hour." His hand moved from the sling to her cheek, his thumb lightly brushing over a bruise that must have come from a flying elbow or hand. "How's Suzanne?"

"Not a scratch." Aaron sniffed in disapproval. "She got exactly what she wanted: a hero." He nodded toward Cade. "And a lot of attention."

The words stung and Cade's back stiffened. "Look, I didn't realize Amy was hurt. If I had known, I would have—"

"Would have what?" Aaron challenged, his voice rising and his aggravation taking the women by surprise. Rilan eased himself on the backside of the sofa and just watched with wide eyes. "You can't see it, man. Suzanne is calculated. Everything she does, every word she says, every move she makes is for her own purpose. I don't believe she aimed to hurt Amy today, but her goal was to have you catch her, dote on her, and to start rumors amongst the students about you two, and you fell for it. And in the process, Amy got hurt."

"Aaron, it's okay." Amy placed a restraining hand on her friend's arm, but Aaron shrugged it away.

"You were seriously hurt, Ames. Suzanne's games have gone too far. If she wants to be dramatic and cause a scene, it cannot be allowed on school property. What if she'd accidentally fallen on a student instead of you? You were collateral damage in her ploy to win attention from Cade. And I'm sorry, it's ridiculous. And it makes me angry to think that she's gloating tonight because she won a date with Cade for her nonsense."

"I agree," Rachel said quietly.

"Whoa, won a date?" Cade asked, bewildered at the idea.

"You're seeing her again, aren't you?" Aaron asked.

Cade felt his face flush at being put on the spot and for being foolish enough to accept Suzanne's dinner invitation as a 'thank you' for helping her.

"Seriously?" Rilan stood to his feet and shook his head in disgust.

"I didn't know she was making it more than it was. She didn't say it was a date. I wasn't going to treat it like one. She wanted to thank me."

"Then why didn't she ask Amy to join you?" Rilan asked, tapping his temple, his own temper flaring. "Use your brain, Uncle Cade. She's playing you."

"Watch your tone with me, Rilan." Cade's harsh tone only stirred his nephew further.

"Whatever. I'm going home." He rested a hand on Amy's shoulder as he walked by her. "Will you have a sub in class tomorrow?"

"Nope. I'll be there," Amy reassured him. "Who else could I trust with a pop quiz?" She winked as if giving him insider knowledge and he smirked, though Cade could tell Rilan's feathers were still ruffled.

"Got it. See you all tomorrow." He walked out, the front door closing with extra force behind him.

Amy closed her eyes and listened to her friends bicker, and Cade noticed she slowly drifted away and toward the hallway to head to the guest room. "Amy, wait—" He bypassed a furious Aaron, but could feel him hot on his heels. Amy held up her hand for the two men to stop their pursuit. "Guys, I'm tired. I want to eat and go to bed. Aaron, I'm not upset about Suzanne. It was an accident. Accidents happen. I'm not upset at Cade." She looked him in the eye. "I'm not. I just want to rest though. I'm sorry if Suzanne was hurt or overdramatic or happy or upset. I don't know, and I don't really care, how she reacted, I'm sorry if she's playing games or not playing games... none of it matters. The day happened. The accident happened. I'm fine. I'm just hungry and worn out. I'm going to crash on Aaron's amazing guest bed tonight and I'll see everyone in the morning at school." She walked down the hall and closed the door.

Cade turned to Aaron and Rachel and placed his hands on his hips. "Look," He shifted under the weight of their disapproving stares. "I'm not interested in Suzanne as more than a friend or colleague. I'll set the record straight if she thinks I am. But sometimes you guys are just as biased against her as she is against you. Let me make up my own mind about people."

"That's fine," Aaron said. "But when our friend gets hurt, we don't sit idly by either. First the car accident and now this…" Aaron paused. "Accidents just seem to befall Amy when she's around you. And I just want it on record that I'm a bit wary of your judgement right now."

Aaron's assessment stung, but Cade took it in stride. He felt like a fool already. Now, he felt like a disappointment, and he didn't like it. He liked Aaron, Rachel, and Amy. He wanted to be friends with them. He hadn't meant for any accidents to happen. And he cared about Amy. Truly cared about her. In fact, if he were to date anyone in his life, he'd choose her, not Suzanne. But how did he let them see that? "I'll see you all tomorrow." He pinched the bridge of his nose and rubbed a hand over the side of his face to try and erase the headache he felt brewing between his eyes. He made his way to the door, pausing a moment when he heard a dish clatter in the kitchen and saw that Amy had reappeared to fix herself a plate of food. His eye caught hers and she gave him a reassuring smile. Every bone in his body ached to walk back in the room to talk with her, but he took his leave as peacefully as he could manage. Tomorrow he'd talk with her. Tomorrow he would straighten out the facts and his feelings toward Suzanne. There'd be no confusion on where his heart and intentions were aimed. Or so he thought.

The next morning, Cade walked across the hall to find Amy standing on a chair trying to tape pieces of railroad tracks on her wall. He noticed several around the room, interrupted by images of buildings, faces, and topics. She stretched on her tiptoes to try and reach above a poster. Cade walked forward and stabilized her as she toppled. She jumped at the touch on her back and relaxed when she saw it was him. "Climbing chairs one-armed, Ms. Frazzle? Seems a bit dangerous."

Amy posted the picture and then stood towering over him by a couple of head lengths. "I like to live on the edge, I guess." She allowed him to help her down and then straightened the front of her blouse and readjusted the strap of her sling. "How are you this morning?"

He shrugged and she lightly patted his shoulder. "They didn't mean it last night, all the nasty comments. They were just emotional about it all."

"I'm pretty sure they meant them," Cade replied. "But it's okay. I get it. They're protective of you, and they should be. You're their friend. And they're right, you do tend to be more accident prone when I'm around."

"You just helped me off a chair," Amy pointed out. "It's not like I'm helping matters. I thought I could catch a woman who is bigger than I am. That's just me not using my better judgment."

"It was you being kind." Cade shoved his hands in his pockets to avoid touching her hair.

"I'd like to think so, but Suzanne showed me her bruised elbow. I'm assuming the one that clocked me here." She pointed to her bruised jaw. "And apparently it was my fault for putting my face in the way." Amy smirked. "I just can't win her over, it seems. So, from here on out, I will just continue to let her be and keep my distance."

Student voices echoed down the halls as the first bell signaled the start of the day. They had five minutes before their classrooms would be flooded with students and he wouldn't be able to chat with her one on one until lunch. "But we're okay, right?" Cade asked. "You aren't going to keep me at a distance, are you?"

Her brow furrowed. "Why would I do that?" Understanding hit her gaze and she nodded. "Ah, right, the face down last night. No. You're my friend. Aaron and Rachel are already over it too. I scolded them this morning. They should never have made it seem like you were in the wrong for helping Suzanne. I'm sorry they did. We're good, Cade, you and me. No hurt feelings, okay?"

"That's good to hear." He reached for the hand that was not draped across her body in the sling and lifted it to his lips. He placed a kiss in her palm. "Good."

"Give me a hug," Amy stepped into his arms and patted him on the back. "Now, get over there and teach those hooligans." She nodded at a few of the students walking into her room, their comments already asking her about her injury. He walked out to her painting the image of her being a swashbuckling buccaneer who'd defeated a kraken sea monster. The next student that asked, he could hear Amy talking about a secret spy mission gone wrong. Smiling that the incident didn't seem to affect her cheerful mood, he jumped as a loud train whistle blew behind him. He turned to find Amy running back across the hall on a giggle as his students laughed at her shenanigans. He heard the whistle three more times before hearing Amy yell, "All aboard the History train!"

∞

Rilan tucked his feet on the book rack beneath the seat of his desk as he fished a sandwich out of his paper sack lunch. He took a hearty bite and then looked up as Amy walked into the room. She paused, changed her exhausted and pain-filled expression to one of cheer, and walked toward her own desk. "When did you sneak in here?"

"A few minutes ago. It okay?"

"Of course." She sat and released a sigh, leaning her head back against her desk chair and closing her eyes a brief moment.

"Your arm hurt?"

"A smidge." She opened her eyes and studied him. "What made you come to eat in my room today? Are you checking up on me?"

"Yes and no," Rilan admitted. "It's homecoming week, so they've been doing loud pep rally style cheers in the cafeteria all week, and it's kind of annoying. And yes, I wanted to check on you." She reached under her desk and opened her mini fridge that had just enough room for her lunch and a few drinks. She pulled out two sodas, tossing one to Rilan, and then setting her own on her desk. She pulled out her plastic container holding leftovers from the supper Aaron and Rachel had whipped together the night before and ate, not even bothered by it being cold. "Did Uncle Cade apologize to you?"

"And what would he need to apologize for?" Amy asked.

"For being stupid."

"I think you're being too hard on him. All of you are. It is not his fault this happened, and he too was just trying to be helpful to Suzanne. He cannot be blamed for her plans, should there be any."

"But did he talk with you? He's not avoiding you because he's embarrassed or anything?"

Amy chuckled. "He is a responsible adult, Rilan, so yes, he came and talked with me this morning. We are coworkers. Even if he wanted to avoid me, he couldn't, and vice versa."

"Yeah, but I'm just making sure he... well, I don't want him to ruin his shot. That's all."

"His shot?" Amy's brow lifted as a knock tapped against the side of her open door. Her jaw dropped at the sight of a large bouquet of flowers being walked inside by the school secretary. "What in the world?" She fished in the flowers for the small card. "Oh my goodness!" She held the card to her heart.

"Who are they from?" Rilan leaned forward and read the card she held out. "Mr. James? How'd he know about your arm?"

"I messaged Peter last night that I wouldn't be going to the assisted living facility this week because of my arm and homecoming, and he must have told his grandpa what happened. Leave it to James to send me the most beautiful flowers I've ever received. He sure does know how to treat a lady."

"Kisses... flowers... what's next? A marriage proposal?" Rilan asked, making Amy wriggle her eyebrows.

"Marriage proposal?" Cade's voice interrupted their conversation and Rilan rolled his eyes at his uncle's timing.

"Amy's." Rilan motioned to the flowers.

"Wow, what did I miss?"

"A lot," Rilan muttered as he gathered up his trash and tossed it into the trash can. He sipped on his soda as Amy narrowed her eyes at him to give his uncle a break. "They're from my boyfriend."

"Wow. I did miss some big news, then."

"He's a great kisser too." Amy snickered and Cade immediately knew who she spoke of.

"James beats me at every turn." His comment took her by surprise, but she played along.

"Oh really? Am I to expect another bouquet of flowers today? If so, I love dahlias." She gave an exaggerated wink before waving Rilan out of his seat to move the heavy vase to the top of her filing cabinet. "Will you help carry those for me after school?" Rilan nodded.

"Well, he can on his way to the gym. We still have floats to help with," Cade reminded his nephew.

"Oh yeah, I've got more roses to make, only this time they're smaller, purple, and have less glitter." Amy beamed. "Thankfully."

"You're still helping with the floats?" Cade asked.

"Of course. A broken wing is no excuse for me not to help out. I'm sure I can at least bug Aaron or Rachel today."

"I'll help you with whatever you need."

"You have your own floats, Mr. Wickerson," Amy reminded him. "And a boss that keeps tabs on you." She laughed at the displeasure on his face. "But if you need an escape, I can play the damsel card and 'need help' with something."

"Without falling out of a window," Rilan added dryly.

"Well, let's hope not. I don't think I can handle another fall just yet." Amy laughed and her face grew serious at Cade's frustrated stance. "We're just playing, Cade. I don't mean anything by it. You can help with whatever you want, even if it is not the float you were originally assigned to. Everyone's just grateful for the extra hands." She patted his arm, and he placed his hand over hers and held it there.

The bell rang and Rilan groaned. "And back to life. Hey, after decorating we should go to Romero's for supper." The hope in his voice made Amy nod before even asking his uncle. "Yes!" he cheered.

"Oh," Amy realized she'd answered for Cade and grimaced. "I'm sorry. I didn't even run it by you. I can't make that decision, kid, but if your uncle is up for it, then sure."

"He's up for it. Right, Uncle Cade?"

Cade looked at his nephew, Rilan giving him a nod of encouragement to take the hint and the obvious help in securing dinner plans with Amy. "Sure. Romero's sounds great."

"I'll have to ride with you guys. I carpooled with Aaron this morning, so I am carless."

"I think we could do that." Cade motioned for Rilan to follow him out of the classroom as students began crowding the hallway to find their way to their next class.

Rilan popped his head in Amy's doorway before departing and smirked. "See you sixth period, Amy."

She waved him onward as she walked to the door to greet her next class, catching Cade's eye across the hall as she did so. His face was serious as if he still wasn't sure where he stood with her, so she flashed him a wink to ease the line in his forehead. His lips tilted into a small smile before a ball of wadded paper pelted him in the back from one of his students. Laughing, Amy watched as he picked it up and sent it sailing to the student it'd come from. The final bell rang, and she sat on her stool at the podium in the front of her room as her students settled in their desks. Just a few more classes, some decorating, and then a wonderful supper with friends. She couldn't wait. And as she peeked another glance across the hall and watched Cade engage in conversation with his students, Amy realized she most looked forward to more time with *him*... looked forward to dinner with *him*. And her heart gave a small tug when he looked over her direction and spotted her watching him. Their eyes held a moment longer, an unspoken buzz traveling from one to the other. Her heart beat a little faster and she found her hands nervous as she finally looked away and situated the papers on her podium. It was going to be an interesting day, she thought.

∞

Arms over their heads holding a support beam, Aaron and Cade waited as two teenage boys drilled above them to anchor the wood in place.

"Look at all the muscles over here," Rachel teased, walking up with Amy, both holding faux greenery. Amy draped vines over her shoulders since she wasn't able to carry as many with one arm.

"And you two look like goddesses." Aaron beamed. "All earthy and beautiful."

"Wow, did he just compliment us, Ames?" Rachel stood dumbfounded.

"Athena, at your service." Amy bowed. "You guys hanging in there?"

One of the boys above dropped a screw and mumbled an apology as he tried to hurry and finish his job so Aaron and Cade could relieve their outstretched arms.

"Barely," Aaron admitted. Amy wriggled her fingers his direction and he twitched. "Don't even think about it Ames, or this board and everyone with it comes crashing down."

She laughed and turned her mirth to Cade and did the same gesture.

"I'm not that tough either," Cade admitted, dodging her first attempt without letting go of the board. She stopped when she heard a cough clear the air. Turning, Suzanne stood behind them, arms crossed, and face carved with a disapproving glare.

"Those vines won't hang themselves." She barked, her eyes narrowing upon Amy.

Rachel's back stiffened and she opened her mouth to reply unkindly, but Amy forced a smile. "You're right. We better get to it. I don't want to be late for my dinner." She shot a shy smile at Cade and walked away, Rachel shooting one last glare at Suzanne on their way to their float. Suzanne lingered long enough to eye Cade and Aaron a moment before hurrying off to boss the next person she could find.

"Dinner?" Aaron asked, raising his eyebrow toward Cade.

"Rilan wanted to go to Romero's tonight with Amy and me."

"Ah." Aaron lowered one arm and shook it to gain blood flow before lifting it back up to hold the board and then doing the same to the opposite. Cade followed suit and felt instant relief.

"I know you probably don't approve, but Rilan did the inviting, not me."

"I didn't say anything," Aaron said.

"You said plenty last night. I know you don't think I measure up and what not," Cade continued.

"I never said that either."

"You basically implied it." Cade reminded him. "You don't trust me with Amy."

"Yeah... I said some pretty harsh things to you, and yet, here you stand. You're a decent guy, Cade. I'm protective of Rachel and Amy. It's just a given. Amy and I go way back, and I sometimes tend to *over* protect her. While I am still mad that you fell victim to the Suzanne game, I do see how much Amy enjoys your company and vice versa. I'm also not an idiot. I can tell you care about her too. I just... I don't want to see Amy get hurt, that's all. She deserves the best." A holler had them looking up and receiving the thumbs up from the two boys who high-fived over their carpentry work. The men lowered their arms and groaned in relief.

"I do care about her," Cade admitted. "And there's something... there between us. I don't know yet what it is, but it's there. I know she feels it too. Today was evidence of that. I caught her looking at me across the hall a few times and there's this energy that just seems to hum when we're around one another. I want to explore that."

"And does she?" Aaron asked.

"Not sure. I haven't mentioned anything to her yet. I was kind of hoping to do that this evening after supper."

"And Rilan?"

"That kid's been wanting me to date Amy from the beginning," Cade chuckled. "But I wanted to take time to settle in, get to know her more, and just be comfortable with our life here."

"Smart move."

"But now," Cade added. "I just want to go for it. I'm tired of games and gossip. I want it to be very clear where my feelings are, and they are not with Suzanne." He glanced over as Amy stood handing vines up to Rachel. Rachel stood on a ladder and draped the greenery over the bow of a ship. When she handed Rachel the last one, Amy walked over to her purse and draped it over her shoulder. She found Rilan and he hurried over to her large flower bouquet and lifted it. As a team, their eyes began searching the gym, and Cade knew they were looking for him. His heart squeezed at seeing them both together and he gave a friendly pat on Aaron's arm. "I think that's my cue."

"Cade," Aaron waited until Cade faced him. "Don't screw it up."

He gave a quick nod and jogged over to Rilan and Amy. When he reached them, he gently cupped Amy's cheek, her eyes lighting in surprise. "You ready?"

She nodded, her eyes curious, as he gently brushed his thumb over her bruised jaw.

"Let's go have some Romero's." Cade nodded for Rilan to lead the way, the teen not hesitating. Cade gently placed a hand at the small of Amy's back as he led her out the doors of the gym and into the parking lot. When he stepped into the fresh air, he inhaled a deep breath and sighed as Amy did the same. They both grinned at the relief of not having to be trapped in a musty gym any longer. "How about some chocolate cake, Ms. Frasier?"

"Why, Mr. Wickerson, you know the way straight to my heart." She playfully batted her eyelashes up at him and laughed.

Before she could slip away to hop into the truck, Rilan standing with the passenger door already open for her, Cade grabbed her uninjured hand and tugged her, twirling her toward him. She stumbled into his chest on a gasp of surprise before she looked up at him. When she did, he covered her mouth with his. Surprise had her back stiffening for a brief moment, before his hand gently cupped her face. He then felt her full surrender into the moment and he relished the thrill of kissing her. He tugged her closer, guiding the kiss into deeper territory but Amy abruptly jumped away. Shocked, she shook her finger at him. "Whoa, whoa, whoa... what was that?" Jittery, she reshouldered her purse and her cheeks stained pink when she saw that Rilan had witnessed the entire encounter. His nephew stood beaming by the truck.

"Amy, I—"

"Cade." She waved away his words. "This is not the place. Let's go." She slid into the truck, avoiding his gaze as Rilan shut her door.

"Nice one, Uncle Cade." Rilan grinned.

Embarrassed, Cade flashed an annoyed glance at his nephew. "Get in the truck. And not a word."

Rilan snickered, and Cade bit back a smile as he hopped into the vehicle and headed to the restaurant.

∞

Romero's beckoned. Chocolate cake beckoned. But Amy couldn't move when Cade finally parked the truck and her favorite place stood in front of her. "Rilan," Amy turned in the seat to face the kid in the backseat. "Why don't you go ahead and get us a table? We'll be right behind you." Rilan's lips twitched as he flashed a quick smirk at his uncle before obediently exiting the truck. When he was inside the restaurant, Amy turned to face Cade. "What were you thinking?" she asked.

"Amy—"

"No. I'm going to talk," she interrupted, turning more in her seat to face him. She unbuckled her seatbelt to fully adjust and then leaned across the center console. Gripping the front of his shirt, she pulled him to her and kissed him, her lips urgent, passionate, and smooth. Cade's fingers combed into her hair, and she melted further and further into him. His cell phone buzzed, and she tugged herself out of his gentle hold. Both were breathless, their eyes never leaving the other. Amy brushed her fingertips over his lips and then shook her head on a light laugh. "Yeah, so we need to talk about this."

"It would seem so." Cade smiled, leaning toward her and gently placing another kiss on her lips. "But let's eat first. We have the rest of the evening to dissect and sort out the details, right?"

"And that's what you want to do? You want to sort things out... with me?"

Cade's eyes narrowed as he studied her. "That's exactly what I want. You?"

She nibbled on her bottom lip before a full smile spread over her face and nodded. "Yes. I believe I do."

Relief flooded through the truck and they both leaned back against their seats on satisfied sighs and then laughed at their joint reaction. Cade reached over and squeezed her hand. "Let me treat you to supper and dessert, Amy. And then, I'd like to take you home with me."

Her eyes widened at his insinuation, and he blushed, stammering over his words. "I didn't mean like that. I meant— Wow... I botched this didn't I? I meant take you home so we could talk. Nothing more. I promise that's what I meant." Flummoxed, he avoided her gaze until she burst into laughter.

"Oh, Cade." She leaned over and kissed his warm cheek. "I like when you're flustered. I knew what you meant," she assured him.

"Good." He let out a relieved laugh and rubbed sweaty palms on his pant legs, the action making her heart puddle even further. "I'm not very good at this. It went a lot smoother in my head."

"I like this way better."

His eyes made their way back to her face leaving tingles along their path towards her lips again. Instead of kissing her, he quickly diverted his attention back to the restaurant. "We should go inside. Rilan's going to wonder where we are."

"I'm pretty sure he knows what is happening," Amy giggled, though she climbed out of the truck and waited at the front of the vehicle for Cade. He reached her side, and she slid her arm around his waist. "Now, Mr. Wickerson, feed me cake and tell me I'm pretty."

Cade looked down at her and smirked. "I'll do you one better, Ms. Frasier. I'll feed you cake and tell you I love you." She startled and stopped in her tracks. "Think on that while we eat, won't you?" He opened the door to the smells of garlic and pasta, Rilan raising his hand from a nearby booth to wave them over. Amy continued to stare up at Cade as he escorted her toward his nephew. When they reached the table, Cade winked at her as he motioned for her to slide into the booth space. He slid in beside her as Rilan attempted to be nonchalant.

"You love me?" Amy asked, not caring whether or not the teenager was privy to their conversation anymore.

"From the moment I first saw you." He cast her a quick glance and she caught his chin in her hand and turned him to face her. "Let's just say I understand James' feelings for his Becca." The waiter walked up to the table, Rilan waving him away as Amy held Cade's face in her hand. "My heart loved you the moment it saw you, Amy. It's odd, really, that feeling of just knowing you've met the person you're meant to be with, and you just have to play it cool and go through the motions of getting to know them, even though you know in the end this moment would happen. Or at least you hope it does. All that to say, I know what Heart's Love means now. My heart loved you instantly. It just took my brain a while to grow comfortable with the idea of it happening so quickly."

Speechless, Amy blinked back tears. "Oh, Cade," she muttered, pressing a kiss to his lips. Tenderness swelled inside of her as Cade pulled away and rested his forehead against hers.

"So maybe we can give this a shot?" he motioned between the two of them and she choked back emotion as she nodded. He kissed her forehead and then reached for his menu. "That should do for now." He draped his arm over the back of their booth and Amy snuggled into his side as they both pretended to review the food options. Amy tilted her head and whispered for his ears only, "I love you too, my heart's love."

The waiter walked up to the edge of the table and Rilan loudly groaned. "Guys! Please! Let us order food and then you can stare at each other with stars in your eyes after."

"So dramatic are teenagers these days," Amy murmured, lightly kissing Cade's lips before handing the menu to the waiter. "Lasagna for us and a slice of triple chocolate cake."

Epilogue

"You have some nerve walking in here and acting nonchalant." James' tone was hard but laced with amusement as he nodded at their joined hands. Amy and Cade eased into chairs across from him as Amy leaned towards him and kissed his cheek in welcome. "It's been a while, James. How are you?"

"More than fine, Amy, more than fine. I'm glad to see your arm is better. No more cast, I see."

"Yes, I'm finally mended."

"And it seems, my boy, that you took the jump finally."

Cade laughed. "I did. Thanks for that advice, by the way."

"Oh, you're more than welcome." James beamed. "It's not every day a special woman like Amy comes along. She's like my Becca through and through. You have to snatch them up quickly."

"I couldn't agree more." Cade gently rubbed a hand down the back of Amy's hair.

"And Amy, you get a package deal with this one." James nodded toward Rilan sitting amongst another group of teens and elderlies playing cards in the assisted living home.

"I do." Amy grinned. "They aren't so bad."

James chuckled and slapped a hearty pat on Cade's back. "Not bad at all, Amy love, not bad at all. She'll take good care of you, son. Good care of you." James motioned for Amy to lean closer to him. "Just remember, Amy, to never let him stop surprising you." He flourished his hands and then flicked his wrist, a small bouquet of flowers bursting forth, Amy gasping in delight. She accepted the flowers as James held his hand out to Cade, and the latter shook it. "I'll teach you that one soon." James' eyes glanced at the flowers again and his expression grew cloudy before looking up to find Amy sitting across from him. "Oh, Becca, my love, I was hoping you would come."

Amy squeezed Cade's hand before leaning toward James. "Hello, James. It's good to see you."

Cade stood to give James time with Amy and walked over to Rilan. He rested a hand on his nephew's shoulder, Rilan laying his hand of cards on the table to stand and walk with him a moment. "Everything okay, Uncle Cade?"

"Yes. Just grateful. I didn't mean to pull you away from your game."

"It's all good. I just had my turn so it will be a while. Ethel takes forever on her turns." He nodded to a woman with brightly painted lips in a floral dress situating her cards over and over again. "Everything okay with Mr. James?"

"He's currently talking with his Becca."

"Ah." Rilan nodded in understanding. "She's pretty great, Uncle Cade."

Cade watched as Amy laughed at James' jokes and gently rested her hand on top of the older man's as he spoke, the simple touch one of love and comfort. "She is, isn't she?"

"One thing though..." Rilan held up his finger and waited for his uncle's full attention.

"What's that?"

"When you marry her, I refuse to call her Mrs. Wickerson at school."

Laughing, Cade gripped the back of Rilan's neck and tugged him to himself in a hug. "Deal, kiddo. Deal. But first, we have to get her to say yes."

"She will. You just have to ask," Rilan assured him. "And call Aaron. Because I may have told him you were planning to ask her today."

Cade's eyes widened. "Amy and I haven't even discussed marriage, Rilan. You can't start telling people—"

"You may not have discussed it yet, but I saw the ring box in your truck console the other day, so you've at least been thinking about it a while."

"Yeah, but I haven't talked with you about it, and then she and I haven't really dis—"

"I say it's fine." Rilan beamed. "And I recommend asking her before we get home." He winked and hurried his way back to his seat.

∞

The drive to Cade's house was quiet, which was the norm after a meeting with James. His stories and his transition from past to present always had a sobering effect on them all, but this drive was too quiet. Rilan avoided eye contact, and Cade kept his eyes on the road and only grunted in agreement to whatever she said. It was odd and uncomfortable. When they pulled up to Cade's house, cars lined the street and Aaron's driveway. "What in the world?" Amy asked. "Why are so many people at Aaron's?"

"Oh, right. He mentioned he was throwing a get together today."

"Not to me." Offended, Amy unbuckled her seatbelt and reached for the door handle. Cade reached out and stopped her. Confused, she looked to him for explanation.

"Rilan, will you give us a minute?"

"*Only* a minute." Rilan grinned, slipped out of the truck, and walked to the porch of Aaron's house and patiently waited.

"What is up with him? He's been acting weird," Amy pointed out. "And so have you. What happened at the assisted living center?"

Cade smirked. "Let's get out of the truck."

"No, I want to know what is going on with you two before I go face down Aaron for not inviting me to whatever party he's decided to throw." Amy crossed her arms, her grumpy mood making Cade laugh. She grew even more irritated at his response.

"Fine. I'll do it right here then."

Amy waved her hand as if awaiting his explanation of his behavior, but her mouth dropped when he reached beneath his seat and withdrew a ring box. "I'd hoped for a little more romantic moment, but it would seem we have other people wanting me to get the ball moving." He nodded toward his nephew who sat waiting for them. He opened the box and the beautiful ring glistened against black velvet. "Amy Frazzle Frasier, I love you. I know we haven't known each other long, but deep down I feel like I've known you for ages. I would be honored to drink milk, eat chocolate cake, dress up as dead presidents, and even learn magic, if it all meant I get to spend the rest of my life with you." He reached for her left hand and rubbed his thumb over the back of her ring finger. "I know I come with a little bonus addition," He nodded Rilan's direction. "But he's assured me he's 'more than okay' with my asking you this."

Amy bit back a sob of happy tears as she waited for him to ask her the one question she ached to hear.

"Amy," Cade kissed the top of her hand. "Will you marry me?"

"I knew the moment you moved in across the hall from me, you were going to be trouble, Mr. Wickerson." Smiling, she kissed him. "Yes. Yes, I will marry you." She felt the ring slide onto her finger as Cade kissed her passionately on the lips. A tap sounded on the passenger window and Amy turned to find Rilan hovering. "Seriously, the kid can't even give us a minute?" she laughed as she opened the door to say the same thing to him. Rilan looked at her hand and then lifted her off her feet and swung her in a circle with a whoop of joy.

When she'd found her feet again, Cade was coming around the front of the truck on a laugh and pointed at Aaron's house. "Our party awaits."

"Our party?" Amy asked.

"Apparently everyone was pretty confident you would say yes." He winked at her, flourished his hands, and a small bouquet of flowers burst into view.

Laughing, Amy linked her arm with his and rested her head on his arm. "How could a girl turn down flowers, a future, and a party? Let's go, boys." She reached for Rilan and draped an arm over his shoulders as they all walked into Aaron's house to joy, celebration, and a wonderful future.

THE SIBLINGS O'RIFCAN SERIES   KATHARINE E. HAMILTON

The Complete Siblings O'Rifcan Series Available in Paperback, Ebook, and Audiobook

Claron

https://www.amazon.com/dp/B07FYR44KX

Riley

https://www.amazon.com/dp/B07G2RBD8D

Layla

https://www.amazon.com/dp/B07HJRL67M

Chloe

https://www.amazon.com/dp/B07KB3HG6B

Murphy

https://www.amazon.com/dp/B07N4FCY8V

THE BROTHERS OF HASTINGS RANCH SERIES

The Brothers of Hastings Ranch Series Available in Paperback, Ebook, and Audiobook

You can find the entire series here:
https://www.amazon.com/dp/B089LL1JJQ

All titles in The Lighthearted Collection Available in Paperback, Ebook, and Audiobook

Chicago's Best
https://www.amazon.com/dp/B06XH7Y3MF

Montgomery House
https://www.amazon.com/dp/B073T1SVCN

Beautiful Fury
https://www.amazon.com/dp/B07B527N57

McCarthy Road
https://www.amazon.com/dp/B08NF5HYJG

Blind Date
https://www.amazon.com/dp/B08TPRZ5ZN

Heart's Love
https://www.amazon.com/dp/B09XBDK8LN

Check out the Epic Fantasy Adventure Available in Paperback, Ebook, and Audiobook

U<small>THE</small>NFADING LANDS

The Unfading Lands

https://www.amazon.com/dp/B00VKWKPES

Darkness Divided, Part Two in The Unfading Lands Series

https://www.amazon.com/dp/B015QFTAXG

Redemption Rising, Part Three in The Unfading Lands Series

https://www.amazon.com/dp/B01G5NYSEO

AND DIAMONDY THE BAD GUY

Katharine and her five-year-old son released Captain Cornfield and Diamondy the Bad Guy in November 2021. This new books series launched with great success and has brought Katharine's career full circle and back to children's literature for a co-author partnership with her son. She loves working on Captain Cornfield adventures and looks forward to book two releasing in 2022.

Captain Cornfield and Diamondy the Bad Guy: The Great Diamond Heist, Book One
https://www.amazon.com/dp/1735812579

Captain Cornfield and Diamondy the Bad Guy: The Dino Egg Disaster, Book Two
https://www.amazon.com/dp/B0B7QGTSFV

Subscribe to Katharine's Newsletter for news on upcoming releases and events!
https://www.katharinehamilton.com/subscribe.html

Find out more about Katharine and her works at:
www.katharinehamilton.com

Social Media is a great way to connect with Katharine. Check her out on the following:

Facebook: Katharine E. Hamilton
https://www.facebook.com/Katharine-E-Hamilton-282475125097433/

Twitter: @AuthorKatharine
Instagram: @AuthorKatharine

Contact Katharine:
khamiltonauthor@gmail.com

ABOUT THE AUTHOR

Katharine started to read through her former paragraph she had written for this section and almost fell asleep. She also, upon reading about each of her book releases and their stats, had completely forgotten about two books in her repertoire. So, she put a handy list of all her titles at the beginning of this book, for the reader, but mostly for her own sake. Katharine is also writing this paragraph in the third person... which is weird, so I'll stop.

I love writing. I've been writing since 2008. I've fallen in love with my characters and absolutely adore talking about them as if they're real people. They are in some ways, and they've connected with people all over the world. I'm so grateful for that. And I appreciate everyone who takes the time to read about them.

I could write my credentials, my stats, and all that jazz again, but quite frankly, I don't want to bore you. So, I'll just say that I'm happy. I live on the Texas Coast, (no ranch living for now), and I have two awesome little fellas, ages six and two, who keep me running... literally. I also say a lot of, "Don't touch that." "Put that back." "Stop pretending to bite your brother." "Did you just lick that?"

Thankfully, I have a dreamboat cowboy of a husband who helps wrangle them with me. I still have my sassy, geriatric chihuahua, Tulip. She may be slowing down a bit, but she will still bite your finger off if you dare try to touch her, the sweetheart. And then Paws, our loveable snuggle bug, who thinks she is the size of a chihuahua, but is definitely not.

That's me in a nutshell.

Thank you for reading my work.

I appreciate each and every one of you.

Oh, and Claron has now sold over 100,000 copies. Booyah!

And Graham is not far behind him. Woooohoooo!

Made in the USA
Coppell, TX
02 June 2023

17624120R00173